P9-CND-967

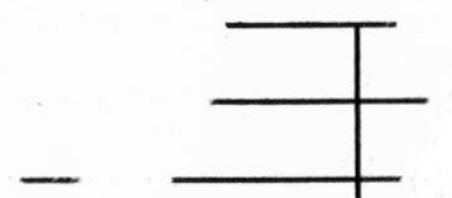

Alice and her grandparents were awakened in the middle of the night. . . .

Alice had not understood all the things that were happening to them. 'What are they going to do with us?' she had asked. And Grandfather, who could always explain everything so well, had said, 'Perhaps we are going to be sent on a long journey.'

'But are we being made *to go on this journey?' Alice had asked. Grandfather had explained that in wartime everything was different from peacetime. The state did not waste time asking the citizens what they wanted. Somewhere in the east they needed people who could work in the fields or factories, and they were sending them there.*

'You and Grandmother, work in the fields?' Alice had asked incredulously. 'You've got that splinter in your knee, and Grandmother has swollen joints and varicose veins and can't lift anything heavy.'

'We shall be some use for something,' Grandfather had said cheerfully. 'And if they can't use us at all, perhaps they will send us home again. . . .'

OTHER PUFFIN BOOKS YOU MAY ENJOY

Anna Is Still Here Ida Vos

Anne Frank: Beyond the Diary
Rian Verhoeven and Ruud Van der Rol

The Devil in Vienna Doris Orgel

The Devil's Arithmetic Jane Yolen

Friedrich Hans Peter Richter

Grace in the Wilderness Aranka Siegal

The Lady with the Hat Uri Orlev

Letters from Rifka Karen Hesse

Mischling, Second Degree Ilse Koehn

A Pocket Full of Seeds Marilyn Sachs

Gudrun Pausewang

The Final Journey

Translated by Patricia Crampton

PUFFIN BOOKS

PUFFIN BOOKS
Published by the Penguin Group
Penguin Putnam Books for Young Readers, 345 Hudson Street, New York, New York 10014, U.S.A.
Penguin Books Ltd, 27 Wrights Lane, London W8 5TZ, England
Penguin Books Australia Ltd, Ringwood, Victoria, Australia
Penguin Books Canada Ltd, 10 Alcorn Avenue, Toronto, Ontario, Canada M4V 3B2
Penguin Books (N.Z.) Ltd, 182-190 Wairau Road, Auckland 10, New Zealand

Penguin Books Ltd, Registered Offices: Harmondsworth, Middlesex, England

First published in Germany by Ravensburger Buchverlag Otto Maier GmbH, 1992
First English-language translation published in Great Britain by Viking, 1996
Published by Puffin,
a member of Penguin Putnam Books for Young Readers, 1998

3 5 7 9 10 8 6 4

Original German title *Reise im August*

LIBRARY OF CONGRESS CATALOGING-IN-PUBLICATION DATA
Pausewang, Gudrun.
[Reise im August. English]
The final journey / Gudrun Pausewang ; translated by Patricia Crampton.
p. cm.
Summary: During World War II, eleven-year-old Alice, whose life has been sheltered and comfortable, discovers some important things about herself and the people she meets when she and her grandfather board a train and begin an increasingly intolerable journey to an unknown destination.
ISBN 0-14-130104-X (pbk.)
1. Holocaust, Jewish (1939–1945)—Juvenile fiction. [1. Holocaust, Jewish (1939–1945)—Fiction. 2. World War, 1939–1945—Jews—Fiction. 3. Concentration camps—Fiction.] I. Crampton, Patricia. II. Title.
PZ7.P2847Fi 1998 [Fic]—dc21 98-16338 CIP AC

Printed in the United States of America

1

•••

The sliding-door of the railway truck closed with a deafening clang. In Alice's memory that sound was the start of the journey, although another half-hour passed before the train left. She felt Grandfather's hand round her own – Grandfather's familiar, big, dry hand. His hand was cold.

The clang brought sudden darkness to the truck. The pale light of the early August morning did not enter. Only stars shimmered in the darkness: six-pointed yellow stars, sewn to coats and jackets. Children cried out, but Alice was silent. Grandfather's hand grasped hers more firmly.

Gradually her eyes became used to the darkness, and now she could see the outlines of people and luggage. A meagre light fell through two gratings high up on the long walls of the truck, but Grandmother would not have been able to thread a needle by it.

Grandmother. How would she be getting on now? Where was she? Outside Alice could still hear the whimpering of the little black dog which had run beside the woman with three children on the march to the station. Barking and whining, it had tried again and again to jump into the truck with them. Then one of the policemen, only a few steps away from Alice, had struck it on the head with his rifle butt. Grandfather had put his hand over her eyes but through his fingers she could see what happened. The dog had done the policeman no harm, and now it lay outside, not yet quite dead.

A metallic screech drowned the feeble whimpering. Iron scraped over iron: someone outside was busy at the truck doors. Men's voices roared orders, then came a jolt that threw Alice against her grandfather. She could feel his elbow by her shoulder.

Feet apart, he braced himself to keep his balance, but in the end he was forced to lean against the wall, against the closed sliding-door. There he stayed, with Alice right beside him.

The train began to move.

'Struppi!' wailed the three children beside her. The youngest began to cry loudly and tears rose in Alice's eyes as well.

'Quietly!' said Grandfather. 'Quietly now.'

The woman beside Alice drew the weeping little boy to her side. It was deathly still in the truck, as if everyone were listening to the bumping sounds moving away from them into the distance, buffer against buffer. The floor of the truck shuddered; the rhythmic snorting of the engine speeded up.

Suddenly a woman screamed. Alice jumped. What the woman was screaming could not be heard over the clanking noises; it sounded strangely far away. She must be in the next truck. Suddenly the screams stopped.

'What's the matter with that woman?' Alice asked her grandfather. Grandfather cleared his throat, something he always did when he found it difficult to answer. What could it mean? Alice had never heard anyone scream like that before. Grandfather squeezed her hand hard, so hard that it almost hurt. Why did he say nothing? She looked up at him. He was so tall that she came up only to the breast pocket of his coat.

Alice was small for her age. Only just now on the platform a woman had taken her for ten, although she was nearly twelve. Grandmother said she thought Alice would have grown more quickly if she had been able to get out in the fresh air more often in recent years. Where they were going now, they would spend a lot of time in the fresh air and she would soon come up to Grandfather's shoulder.

Oh, Grandmother, dear, darling Grandmother! She must be so worried now. She and Grandfather were so close that it was impossible to imagine either without the other. And she, Alice, was part of the closeness.

On the platform Grandfather had asked again and again for the Transport Officer. A policeman had pointed to a man in a black uniform. Grandfather shouted to the man over the heads of all the people waiting that his wife was missing – he could not go without his wife . . . but the Transport Officer had looked through Grandfather as if he were not there. Up to the last minute, Grandfather went on gazing down the platform at the road along which the lorry Grandmother had been standing in had disappeared. They had had to wait almost an hour, but still Grandmother had not come back.

Alice was freezing and she pressed close to Grandfather. What a good thing Grandmother had made her put on her coat, although the sleeves were a little tight now.

'Grandfather,' whispered Alice, rubbing her cheek against his arm, 'will she come on the next train?'

'Yes,' murmured Grandfather, 'on the next train . . .'

He pulled out his big white handkerchief and blew his nose for a long time. Grandmother had ironed those handkerchiefs the day before yesterday.

Alice could feel herself getting more and more tired. She

had had to get up so early. She slipped her bulging rucksack off her back and put it down on the floor beside her. A baby cried. It belonged to the blonde young woman who had been the first to climb into the truck. The woman had another child too, a little boy of about three, with fair, curly hair. He too was beginning to fret.

'Do you want to sleep, Mousie?' asked Grandfather. He pushed the holdall towards her, big as a suitcase but more comfortable to sit on. Alice nodded and sank down on to it, leaning against Grandfather's leg.

Rat-tat-tat, rat-tat-tat. Alice closed her eyes. In earlier days they had sometimes gone by train to visit Aunt Irene and Uncle Ludwig, a journey of barely half an hour. Uncle Ludwig was a cattle dealer who always had new horses and cows in his stables, and you could smell the stable smell even in the living-room. Alice remembered Aunt Irene's peals of laughter, the crowds of children from the village who ran through the stables, the swallows' nests on the house walls and the hens in the orchard.

If only the train were going there now. But Uncle Ludwig and Aunt Irene had gone away a long time ago and had not come back.

2

Alice could not sleep. She opened her eyes and looked at the floor: thick, black muck filled in the gaps between the planks, and it was on this floor that people were sitting.

She felt her stomach rise. The truck did not smell good either. Just beside her sat the woman with the three children whom the dog Struppi had run after. The children, two boys and a girl, leaned against their mother, their faces streaked with tears. Behind them, in the middle of the truck, a family squatted on their luggage: parents, grandparents and a number of children. The mother was just distributing little pieces of unleavened bread. An older boy put his own cracker on the floor while he fed his little brother.

Alice tugged at her grandfather's sleeve. 'That boy is putting his matzoh on the dirty floor . . .'

The mother of the three children laughed. Alice looked at the woman, shocked. Did the dirt not matter to her? Dirt disgusted Alice. Even as a little girl she had always wanted to change immediately if she made herself messy at table or in a game. 'Don't bring the child up so fussy,' Aunt Irene had said from time to time. 'Children have to get dirty sometimes.'

But in the matter of cleanliness Mummy and Grandmother had no sense of humour.

'Don't laugh,' said Grandfather harshly. 'Leave the child alone.'

'And what are you going to tell her when she realizes that there are no lavatories when you travel in this class?' the woman retorted.

A few seconds passed before Alice understood.

'Is it true, Grandfather?' she asked, shaken.

'Have a little sleep, child,' he replied.

What did it mean? Why was he trying to put her off? Alice stood up and Grandfather put his arm round her shoulders.

'We're going to get to know each other on this journey better than we care to,' said the woman, so quietly that Alice could scarcely hear her. Then she introduced herself. Her name was Ruth Mandel and her children's names were David, Ruben and Rebekka.

'Dubsky,' said Grandfather. 'Siegfried. And this is Alice, my granddaughter.'

Meanwhile, a quarrel had flared up in the back left-hand corner: a husband and wife, sitting on their cases, had been asked to leave the corner. The young man with brown, curly hair who was trying to persuade them became more and more insistent. Soon Alice realized what they were talking about: the corner was to be used as a lavatory. The two people on the case were wearing trench coats, the kind that Daddy used to wear.

'Well, why here, then?' shouted the woman. 'There are three other corners.'

'In one of them,' cried the young man, growing angrier all the time, 'is a heavily pregnant woman, in another a woman with two small children, and in the third two old, sick –'

'We're sick too,' the man in the trench coat interrupted him.

'Do be sensible and consider,' said a tall, grey-haired man quietly. 'In this situation we shall manage only if we try to get on with each other.'

The young man grasped the case and tugged it out of the corner. The couple tried furiously to stop him, and one or two people sitting round them got up. Another man and the baby's mother waded in and took the young man's side. Mrs Mandel jumped up and stood in front of her children, who were in danger of being trampled by the struggling group.

Then the blonde young woman with the curly-headed child pushed her way into the corner. She twitched the little fellow's trousers down and held him out. Then she took a roll of toilet paper from her skirt pocket. When she left the corner the trench-coat couple moved away without argument.

There was complete silence in the truck. The people who had been closest to the Trench-coats also moved a little further from the corner and the Mandels moved up very close to Alice and her grandfather.

'Grandfather,' whispered Alice.

Grandfather gently turned her face towards him.

'How long will this journey last?' she asked miserably.

'Not long, Mousie.'

'A day and a night,' said Mrs Mandel. 'I heard it from one of the train guards.'

'Please,' said Grandfather, and Alice noticed that his voice trembled. Mrs Mandel was tall and slim, with smooth brown hair pulled back to the nape of her neck and a short fringe. Alice found her hairstyle most unusual. The eyebrows, which almost grew together above her nose, and the fine hair on her upper lip reminded Alice of Miss Krockhoff, who had given her piano lessons a long time ago, in the days when everything was still all right. Alice was astonished to hear the children calling their mother 'Ruth'. How extraordinary! She would never have thought of calling Mummy 'Lilli' or Daddy 'Leo'.

Then a little girl with a pink ribbon in her hair was taken to the corner by her mother. She crouched and her mother stood in front of her.

On the other side of the truck three elderly women were unpacking cheese sandwiches. Most were given to a podgy man sitting between them, who seemed younger than the women. He had short, stubbly hair, and his friendly grin he reminded Alice of a child. He stuffed the sandwiches into his mouth so greedily that she could not bear to watch him.

'Would you like something to eat?' she heard her grandfather ask. Alice shook her head violently. The very thought of food made her feel sick, and in any case she had already eaten an oatcake on the platform.

What an extraordinary platform that was. Not like the one they left from to visit Uncle Ludwig and Aunt Irene, but quite a distance from the station, on a siding between sheds and warehouses. And there had been so many people there, more than she had seen for years – all crowded tightly together and surrounded by policemen. And the little black dog had tried again and again to reach the Mandels, but each time the police had chased him off.

There was a disturbance near the other sliding-door. The door had not slid right home and a man was trying to pee through the finger-wide opening. He was standing just beside the three ladies who were eating with their plump companion. All they could do was move away a little from the opening.

'Ruth – I've got to go too,' whispered David, the youngest Mandel, who Alice thought was five or six years old. His mother gave him paper and let him go alone. Suddenly it was pitch dark.

'A tunnel!' cried Ruben.

Once again nothing but the yellow stars were visible, brighter than the first time, Alice thought. But there were fewer of them, because many people had taken off their coats. Others were sitting with their knees drawn up, hiding the stars on their chests. By now most of the people in the truck were sitting down. It was impossible to stand comfortably unless you could lean against the walls, because there was nothing to hold on to.

'Ruth,' came a cry from the corner.

'Stay where you are, David,' Ruth Mandel called. 'It will be light again in a moment.'

Children cried. The medley of voices grew louder.

There was a smell of smoke. In the tunnel the sounds of the train were louder, but duller. Alice pressed against her grandfather. It really was pitch dark. She had fortunately stopped being afraid of tunnels very early, on a journey to Nice, when Daddy had held her in his arms when the train windows grew dark.

The semi-darkness returned, the smell of smoke vanished and David returned from the corner, looking relieved. Alice saw that he was wiping his right hand. Ruth Mandel handed him a damp cloth from their luggage and he wiped his hand thoroughly.

Alice caught sight of his feet. That little brown lump sticking to the edge of his left shoe – wasn't it . . .?

She had to be sick.

3

•••

She gave a cry of distress and stood still with her feet apart, head bowed forward and eyes closed. She heard a shrill 'Eeee!', felt Grandfather's hand on her hair and a soft white cloth against her face. It must be the white handkerchief he was using to wipe her mouth. She opened her eyes a little. Now Grandfather was trying to clean the edge of her coat and his right trouser leg. With embarrassment, she realized that the Mandel boys had moved away from her. Ruth tore strips off her roll of paper, wiped the splashes off Alice's shoes and rubbed the floor clean. Grandfather thanked her.

Alice pointed with disgust at the brown lump on David's shoe.

'So that was it,' said Ruth, and, smiling at Alice, she cleaned David's shoe and took the dirty paper to the corner.

Alice scarcely dared to look up, she was so ashamed.

'It could happen to anyone,' said Ruth. 'And here in particular.' Grateful for her comfort, Alice sank down again on the luggage, still weak at the knees.

'Everything is all right now, Mousie,' Grandfather

murmured in her ear. 'But there's still such a smell,' whispered Alice.

'We're sure to be able to wash at the next stop,' he soothed her. Then he unlaced her rucksack and took out the Thermos. He unscrewed the top, poured black coffee into it and gave it to Alice. She made a face. The coffee tasted horrible, but it took away the even more horrible taste in her mouth. She had never been allowed to drink coffee at home; her grandmother had always said it was not healthy for children. All the same, Alice had sipped Grandfather's cup secretly from time to time.

'Only one swallow,' she heard him say now. 'It's very strong.'

Grandfather took the Thermos top from her hand and drank the rest himself. Then he screwed it down tight again and put the Thermos back in the rucksack.

'This coffee was meant for Grandmother as well,' he said sadly. Alice felt her heart beating faster. She did not want to remember what had happened. She wanted to watch and listen to the Mandels.

Ruben must be in the third or fourth class, and Rebekka was probably fourteen. She had long, dark plaits and Alice kept on meeting her eyes, without daring to speak. For the last year or two she had always been alone, but she had wanted so much to talk to children of her own age and play with them. Now that she had the chance, she could not speak. She did not understand herself.

Grandfather sighed. Was his knee hurting again? Alice was used to that. Whenever he had to stand for a long time, the splinter in his knee bothered him – the shell splinter from the First World War. But perhaps he was sighing because he was thinking about Grandmother . . .

Pictures of the last few hours passed before Alice's eyes· how she and her grandparents had been led in a long procession from the waiting-hall to the station. About a thousand people, Grandfather thought. Guards had urged the procession forward in low voices – as if nobody in the town was supposed to be woken up. But she, Alice, needed no urging. She skipped along in the column, because she had only her own rucksack to carry and she was so glad to have escaped at last from the cramped basement flat.

Grandfather had marched quickly too, although he was carrying the suitcase and his heavy winter coat. Only Grandmother was too slow, always holding up the people behind her. It was a long time since she had walked far anywhere and she had varicose veins, and swollen joints as well. About half-way, Grandfather and another man had hoisted her up under the arms and carried her along, but in the end the guards noticed her. They pulled her out of the column and lifted her into the lorry which was being driven behind the procession. An old man who was struggling for breath had also been pushed into the lorry, and the same thing happened to a young girl who had been making all kinds of fuss: at the beginning of the march she had tried, laughing loudly, to leave the column and walk off into a park or a side-street.

'A mental case,' Grandfather had whispered. 'Don't look.'

At the very beginning Alice had noticed the little black dog running beside the column, wagging its tail. The Mandel children had encouraged it lovingly – probably hoping that it would come with them.

At first Grandfather had been glad that Grandmother did not have to walk so far. The lorry was driving behind the column all the time. But when at last they reached the siding between the sheds and warehouses it suddenly drove away, still filled with people. Grandfather wanted to run after it, but the guards ordered him back into the column with loud shouts and threatening gestures. He was in despair.

Grandmother had nothing with her but her handbag.

'Then she'll just go home again,' Alice suggested. 'She had everything she needed at home, didn't she?'

Grandfather had laughed bitterly. 'Home? Did you say *home*?' Then he took a deep breath and spoke as calmly and quietly as ever. 'Of course, Alice. She will go home. Why didn't I think of that myself?'

Alice was beginning to sweat. She took off her coat, laid it over the bag and sat on it. Then she leaned back and closed her eyes.

So now she was sitting in one of those trains that she had sometimes heard Grandmother and Grandfather talking about very quietly, when they thought she was asleep. One of those trains in which so many good friends and acquaintances of her parents and grandparents had gone away. And Lilli, Sarah and Lotte from her own class. And Aunt Irene and Uncle Ludwig too. All of them had gone away, no one had ever come back. How strange.

'Grandfather,' she whispered, 'why do we have to travel like this, in a train without seats and lavatories? When we went to Nice –'

'There's a war on,' Grandfather interrupted her hastily. 'Everyone has to put up with things.'

Ruth gave Grandfather an angry look. It seemed to Alice that Ruth could not stand him, but what he had said explained everything.

A beam of reddish, very bright light, in which dust specks danced, now shone through one of the two gratings. As the light moved, it touched one or two faces. Alice was astonished at the warm light; it was so long since she had seen the sun. It had never shone down into the basement flat, only for a short time at noon into the well in front of the windows.

The sunlight rested for a while on a middle-aged woman, her chestnut-coloured hair carefully done, shining in the half-light. She had several necklaces round her neck, and golden earrings which looked like Mummy's. The most beautiful necklace sparkled like a rainbow and flashed with light. Alice could not take her eyes off it.

The woman was wearing a red, frilly dress, and over her shoulders hung a black fur coat, all tiny curls. Grandmother had also brought a coat like that with her. She had it with her wherever she went. It was called Persian lamb. Once Grandfather had called Grandmother 'my Persian lady'. That had been a long time ago, when they had gone for a walk in the park one winter's day. Alice had jumped round and round Grandmother, shouting 'Persian lady, Persian lady'.

This woman's shoes, with their very high heels, reminded her of Mummy's shoes. Did the wonderful scent that occasionally reached Alice's nose come from her? Mummy used to smell like that too. Later on, in the basement flat, she and Grandmother had sometimes talked longingly about different perfumes, breathing through their noses and saying '*Aaah*!', although there was nothing but stuffy basement air to smell.

The Persian lady sat straight on her case, beautiful and imperious as a queen. She did not fit in here in this truck at all. Most of the passengers had lowered themselves on to their luggage by now; only a few men were still standing by the gratings, calling out the names of the stations through which the train passed. The names meant nothing to Alice. She glanced at the cases, bags and baskets. Most of them had been packed with care and thought, and bore the names of their owners on the front or side in finger-length letters. Alice glanced at their own travelling bags, which had both Grandmother's and Grandfather's names on them, painted in large letters on the leather. In the excitement of the last few hours she had not noticed that at all.

She began to think. Painting letters like that took time, but they had been given only a few minutes to get ready to leave. Grandmother could not possibly have painted the names in so short a time, so they must have been on the case before then. That meant that her grandparents had been expecting this journey. Then she remembered the fat soldier who had taken them away in the night – that remark about the bag.

The grey-haired man forged his way across the truck and introduced himself as Arnold Blum. He had been a dealer in antiquities. He spoke so loudly that everyone could hear him; no one knew how long the journey might last and what would happen on it, so it might perhaps be useful to draw up a list of the people in this truck, and Mr Blum offered to do this.

People agreed; someone even clapped. So he climbed over the luggage with paper and pencil, worked his way through the truck and noted name, age and home address.

Alice listened attentively. She very much wanted to know the names of the people who were taking this long journey with her. She had always been very good at picking up names, better in fact than Mummy and Daddy or her grandparents. Mr Blum had just reached the woman in the Persian coat and asked politely for her name. She did not react. Perhaps she was asleep. When Mr Blum touched her shoulder, she threw back her head and said roughly, 'What am I to you? What are you to me? What is all this to me?'

Quietly, Mr Blum said, 'Sorry,' and left her in peace.

'Forty-nine,' he reported, adding, 'Fifteen men, seventeen women and seventeen children.'

'My God,' said somebody.

'Grandmother would have been the fiftieth,' sighed Grandfather.

Alice heard his voice, as if from a great distance, saying, 'In the war the maximum load was forty men per cattle truck.'

But her eyes were already closing.

4

•••

Rat-tat-tat, rat-tat-tat. The rhythm of the train found its way into Alice's dreams. She was just opening a big window, leaning out and seeing nothing but an infinite sea. Then came a loud, persistent hissing. The rhythm slowed, the *rat-tat-tat* fell silent, the trucks jolted against each other. She heard someone say, 'Probably no platform ready.'

The sea dissolved, the light faded, space shrank. Once again Alice was sitting in the half-light of the cattle truck. The beam of light was now painting a triangle in rather deeper colours on the plank wall above the lavatory corner.

Alice saw Grandfather's legs drawn up beside her, a bit of hairy skin visible between crumpled socks and trouser bottoms. Her grandfather was no longer standing but was sitting beside her on the floor. He had folded the thick coat carefully and used it to sit on.

Alice was astonished. Up to now she had always seen her grandfather sitting on chairs. Earlier, when they had still gone for walks, he had taken a shooting-stick seat with him if they were going far. Or he would sit on a park bench. He had always been worried about getting dirty. And then, the ants.

Even the night before, in the waiting-hall, he had not sat on the straw. Now he was sitting there on the floor, like a child. It was a good thing Grandmother could not see him.

Alice looked affectionately at her grandfather. He was so big and strong, although he was already sixty-two. He could throw a ball further than Daddy! And finger-wrestling, just for fun, he had pulled Daddy across the table. But he could not stand up for long, because of the splinter.

Now his face was so sad: rings under the eyes, deep lines from his nostrils to the corners of his mouth. He must be thinking of Grandmother. Alice stroked his knee cautiously.

Someone trod on her foot. Everyone was crowding towards the gratings to peer out, and one of them was just beside Grandfather. The young man with the brown, curly hair was standing there, the one who had been so angry when the trench-coat people did not want to give up their corner. He lifted the children up and let them look through the grating. They called him Paul. The father of the two little girls with hair ribbons also came to the grating and threw out a letter. Alice had seen him writing all the time – on his knees. His wife, sitting a few metres away from Alice, had other letters in her hand. How young she was, but her lenses were so thick you could scarcely see her blink behind them.

'There's no one here,' said Paul. 'We've stopped in the open.'

'There's always a chance,' said the letter-writer.

He was broad and short, but it seemed to Alice that he had once been fat. His suit hung loosely, his cheeks were slack. His name was Benjamin Grün, as he had told Mr Blum.

Alice asked her grandfather to lift her up to the grating as well, but he would not. If the train had stopped in the open there would be nothing to see anyway, and he did not want to face the difficulty of standing up.

Beside her Ruben pushed his way to the wall and tried to

peep between his hands through a crack. Alice turned round too, knelt on the bag and looked for a crack in the wall. Then, just where her own right shoulder had rested, she found a knothole.

'Heavens,' said Ruben, 'are you lucky!'

She closed one eye and pressed the other to the hole. For the first moment she was dazzled, but then the circular image cleared: hilly meadows, a haystack, the edge of a wood with the long shadows of morning. Then a man in uniform with a gun on his belt strode in front of it. The gravel beside the rails crunched under his boots.

'Let me have a go,' said Ruben, pushing her to one side.

She would never have been allowed to behave like that. *Politeness first!* she had learned. And *Always wait your turn!* And *What's mine is mine and what's yours is yours!* She looked sideways at Grandfather, but he had not noticed that Ruben had pushed her away from the knothole. He was staring vacantly ahead.

There was not a breath of air. The truck grew hot and a strong smell came from the corner. Alice held her nose and breathed with her mouth open – one of Grandfather's remedies, if there was no other way of avoiding revolting smells.

Suddenly the woman's voice from the next truck could be heard again. This time they could understand what she was screaming: 'Lia, darling, Lia, my little Lia!'

'Who's she shouting for?' asked David, sitting at Alice's feet.

'For her child,' said Ruth. 'Perhaps she was put in another truck.'

Alice stared at her in horror. How could that have happened? What kind of man could do something like that to a mother and child? How the mother must be longing for her child, and by now the little girl would certainly be crying for her mother. Alice imagined her looking like the curly-headed child, who was now sitting on the lap of the white-haired woman beside the blonde. Was she his grandmother? Alice thought she remembered this woman calling out 'Zilly Herz' to Mr Blum. She had a sweet face, like Grandmother's, but broader and without Grandmother's droopy cheeks.

Now David was pushing his way to the knothole, as if hoping to see the screaming mother face to face. After a time he stepped back, disappointed. Ruben took his place, while David leaned against his mother and started to cry again. Ruth drew him close to her and stroked him. 'Struppi is sure to be dead now, and all the dead are happy,' she said softly.

Alice listened, craning her neck. She had never heard anything like that about dead people. The woman in the next truck was screaming so loudly that she had already made herself hoarse.

Then the blonde with the baby pushed her way across and tried to open the sliding-door against which Alice and Grandfather were leaning. But it remained closed, however hard she rattled it.

'Those damned dogs,' she shouted. 'They've locked us in!'

'What did you expect?' asked the trench-coat man drily.

'Water,' cried the blonde. 'I need water for the children.'

Alice listened. They would come now at any moment, open the door and pass in a bucket full of water so that the blonde could wash her baby and the curly-haired child. Perhaps there would be enough for her too. Just to wash her hands. She felt so grubby.

'You can look again now,' said Ruben, sitting on the floor beside David.

Alice put her left eye to the knothole. Two uniformed men were standing quite close beside it, smoking. They were looking this way and that, laughing and talking. One of them was still young, the other probably not much younger than

Grandfather. Both looked well fed. They were not looking in Alice's direction and they obviously had no intention of opening the sliding-door. Close to tears, the blonde woman returned to her place. The woman in the next truck was still screaming.

'Shut your trap, slut!' roared the younger of the two men. Snatching his gun from his shoulder, he disappeared from Alice's view. Shortly afterwards she heard loud blows from the direction of the next truck. Wood on wood. The screams broke off, began again, briefly and shrilly, and then fell silent, as if someone had clapped a hand over the woman's mouth. The uniformed man returned to the circular knothole, his gun back on his shoulder.

'Did you hear, Grandfather?' whispered Alice.

'Get a little sleep,' he replied, pressing her head to his chest. 'You scarcely managed any before.'

'*Everyone* heard,' she said, twisting away from his arm.

'Sleep, Mousie,' he murmured, turning his head away.

But it was impossible for Alice to sleep. She wanted to know what was going on outside. Once again she put her eye to the knothole, and saw the two uniformed men disappearing in opposite directions. The sound of their footsteps faded. Then the engine whistled, the train jerked, and haystacks and woods passed out of sight.

It was a strain, kneeling bent over. Alice turned round and leaned against the wall so that she was covering the knothole with her shoulder. It was *her* knothole!

Now the blonde woman was talking to one or two other women near her. Weeping loudly, she cried, 'She's wearing me out. I haven't got that many napkins with me.'

Alice cast a quick look at the lavatory corner. The heap had grown. A dirty napkin lay on the floor nearby. A boy from the big family was just squatting in the corner. Alice sniffed involuntarily, but could smell nothing. The draught of the train must be sucking out the stench through the cracks and gratings.

She remembered the toilets in the waiting-hall. They had spent three hours in that hall the night before, from one to four. Grandmother and Grandfather had refused to lie down on the wet straw; both had spent the whole time sitting on their case. For a time they had sat back to back, then side by side again. Once they had dropped off for a little, then exchanged a few words. Grandmother had cried quietly. The bright ceiling lights had disturbed Alice a lot, and it felt so odd, sleeping in her coat. Grandfather had spread his own coat over her as well. They had been almost alone in the huge hall. So much room – after so long in the crowded basement. But in the end, despite all the excitement, she had fallen asleep after all.

Towards morning Grandmother had woken her gently and tenderly. Alice had been astonished to see that by now the hall was full of people. Not all of them had found somewhere to lie on the straw, many had not even found a space to sit in, and all of them, except for the little children, had that yellow star on their chests.

'Why are they all wearing those stars?' Alice had asked.

'All Jews have to wear them,' Grandmother explained.

'Then why don't *we* wear stars?' was Alice's next question.

'You have to wear them only in the street,' said Grandfather. 'We never went out of the house.'

'Mummy and Daddy didn't have any stars either, when they went to the dentist,' cried Alice.

But then there was confusion; the whole hall had turned into a seething anthill. No more time for talk.

'In a quarter of an hour we'll be off to the station,' Grandfather had said, helping her on to her feet. Grandmother had quickly sent her to the lavatory again. 'Just in case, because you never know what the sanitary conditions will be like on the train.'

The lavatory had been dreadfully dirty and Alice had felt sick all the time. When she washed her hands in the equally filthy wash-basin, a policeman came into the lobby, thundered on the doors of the cabins and chased out everyone who was still there. 'Pack of swine!' he had roared.

Alice was scared to death. Why was the policeman so nasty?

'He is overworked,' Grandfather explained.

Soon after four everyone was marched out of the hall. Uniformed men with guns over their shoulders accompanied the long procession. Alice's sickness soon vanished with the cool air. She felt better than she had felt for a long time. It was still dawn and Alice could not stop looking up. So much sky!

She had never been outside so early in the morning before. The procession walked almost silently through the empty, silent town. Only the black dog barked from time to time, and the crescent moon was still hanging over the trees in the park.

Wonderful moon! From the basement windows she had scarcely ever been able to see it. As they walked to the station it had paled slowly.

5

Someone climbed over Alice. She made herself small and pulled in her feet. In the whole truck Paul was the only one still standing. At irregular intervals he called out place-names, repeating them patiently if anyone asked. Most of the names meant nothing to Alice, only a few sounded familiar. Perhaps they had once been the answers in Grandmother's crossword puzzles. The grown-ups listened attentively to Paul. Fulda – Bad Hersfeld – Eisenach. Mr Blum had a small map on his knee.

'Do you think we'll be there soon?' Alice asked her grandfather, who shook his head sadly.

'And if we really have to go on travelling through the night,' she said, 'what will happen then? There is no light in the truck.'

'Don't worry,' said Grandfather. 'I put in a big torch.'

Grandfather always thought of everything.

David and Ruben were getting lively. Had they already forgotten the black dog? They were playing a game which made them laugh. Keeping time, each took off the other's cap and put it on his own head, getting faster and faster.

Sometimes the caps landed askew on their heads, covering one eye or both, until Alice had to laugh too. But when her eyes met Grandfather's grave ones, she tried to be serious. Only it was not so easy. Ruben was making such funny faces, she had to look away in order not to burst out laughing.

'Laugh, children, laugh,' said Ruth. 'Feel free.'

Mr Grün was still writing, bowed over his knee. His wife held the finished letters in her hand. Then she stood up and made her way across to the other grating. When Paul called out the name of a station she pushed one letter through the grating. Alice wanted to ask Grandfather why she was doing it, but he had fallen asleep.

On the other side the blonde woman had unbuttoned her blouse and was holding the baby to her breast to feed. Alice stared. How greedily the baby drank. Alice stood up and made her way over to them.

'Well,' said the blonde, 'do you want to stroke her?'

Alice touched the fuzzy little head, then stroked it cautiously. In the last two years she had seen babies only in pictures, and bigger children too, and adults. The only people she mixed with in real life were her parents, her grandparents and Mrs Lohmann.

She noticed that everything had grown quiet; everyone was looking at her, stroking the baby. She looked across at Grandfather, but he was still asleep. What a pity. She would have loved to tell him how wonderful she found this tiny child.

When she went back to her place, she thought of her mother. Her mother had once explained to her: 'When a man and a woman love each other very much, a new life starts under the wife's heart. The little creature grows in her body for nine months until it sees the light of the world . . .'

Alice could see into the right-hand corner on her own side only if she moved away from the wall a little. There sat the thin, pale woman with the big stomach. She had loved a man so much that a child had grown under her heart.

'Gotha!' cried Paul. Mrs Grün dropped a letter through the grating. David pushed his way over to Paul and asked to have a look out. Paul lifted him up, the wind of their passage making his brown curls flutter. David clung to the bars of the grating and peered out.

'Sheep, lots and lots of sheep,' he cried. 'And there is a black dog with them.' For a moment he was quiet, then he burst into tears. Paul put him down and comforted him. Ruben wanted to be lifted up as well, then came a little boy from the big family. The two little girls with the pink ribbons wanted to look out too. Paul had a lot to do.

Alice would also have liked to look through the grating, but Grandfather was still asleep. Should she just do it?

'Want a go?' asked Paul. Could he read thoughts? Alice jumped to her feet and let herself be lifted up in the air. A fresh, warm wind stroked her hair and cheeks. What a wonderful feeling! From outside, the scent of hay and camomile blew in. Daisies and corn poppies sparkled on the embankment. A little girl was swinging in the garden of a level-crossing-keeper's house. She had long, dark hair, just like Alice. Alice quickly put her hand through the bars and waved, and the girl on the swing waved back.

Paul lifted her down again and Alice thanked him. When she went back to her place, the corner smelled more disgusting than before, and Alice suddenly could not understand how she had put up with the stench for so long. Now the old woman from the big family was squatting in the corner; her husband was holding up a coat as a makeshift curtain. Their name was Maibaum. There were ten Maibaums in the truck.

Alice dropped on to the holdall and looked across at Paul. He was tall and slim, with a very friendly face, and those brown curls – how well they suited him!

One of the men who had come to take them away in the night had had curls like that. He had looked like a prince, or a young Greek from Grandfather's art book. The other had been short and fat and worn glasses.

They had come after midnight, when the family had been fast asleep and heard nothing. Grandmother and Grandfather had not woken her until they themselves were already dressed and ready to go. Grandfather had handed her clothes to her one by one, while she dressed. In the kitchen a strange man's voice had shouted, 'Get on with it. There's more people waiting to be picked up tonight.' A second man's voice had laughed. Then the one with the loud, razor-sharp voice had thundered upstairs to get Mrs Lohmann out of bed as well. She had probably been woken up by the noise long before. After all, the basement was usually so quiet.

The fat man with the glasses who had laughed had stayed in the kitchen. He had more patience than the other, even when Grandmother had not been able to find her pills right away. He had stroked Alice's hair and murmured, 'Poor little thing.' And to Grandmother he had said, 'I've got a daughter her age too.' But then, grinning, 'Already expecting it, eh? Yes, they'll all be found. Sooner or later.'

'And where,' Grandmother had asked, her voice shaking, 'are you taking us?'

'Where, Madam? To the east, everyone to the east.' Then that grin again. He had led them up the stairs to the front door, out to the lorry with the barred windows. When Grandmother could not manage the steps right away, he had taken her by the waist and lifted her up. After all, she was only 'a little half-person', as Grandfather always said.

Shortly afterwards Mrs Lohmann had appeared at the front door. She was the present owner of the house which had once belonged to Grandmother and Grandfather. Her husband and Grandfather had been old soldiers together. Mr

Lohmann had received the highest order for courage, which his wife was always glad to show people.

Mr Lohmann had been a professional soldier, but after the war they had not needed officers any more and he had become a shareholder in Grandfather's wholesale coffee business. They had always got on splendidly. Soon after Alice's seventh birthday he had died suddenly, and she had been allowed to go to the funeral. It had been a very big occasion, with a lot of officers, a lot of speakers and a lot of banners. Afterwards Mrs Lohmann had taken over the shares. Grandfather and Daddy had worked with her very well – until war broke out and the wholesale coffee business had been closed down. It was scarcely possible to get coffee from anywhere then.

Mrs Lohmann was a tall, dignified woman, and even now as she walked out of the front door she looked very elegant. But then Alice saw that she was wearing her dress back to front, and when the curly-haired man pushed her into the lorry with the Dubskys, she was shaking all over. And when the lorry stopped outside the waiting-hall and Mrs Lohmann tried to get out behind Grandmother, the curly-haired man waved her back: she was to be taken somewhere else. She could give them only a quick wink of acknowledgement.

'That will upset her,' said the fat man, leading the three Dubskys into the hall. 'As the wife of a highly decorated officer –'

Alice had not understood all the things that were happening to them. 'What are they going to do with us?' she had asked. And Grandfather, who could always explain everything so well, had said, 'Perhaps we are going to be sent on a long journey.'

'But are we being *made* to go on this journey?' Alice had asked. Grandfather had explained that in wartime everything was quite different from peacetime. The state did not waste time asking the citizens what they wanted. Somewhere in the east they needed people who could work in the fields or the factories, and they were sending them there.

'You and Grandmother, work in the fields?' Alice had asked incredulously. 'You've got that splinter in your knee, and Grandmother has swollen joints and varicose veins and can't lift anything heavy.'

'We shall be some use for something,' Grandfather had said cheerfully. 'And if they can't use us at all, perhaps they will send us home again . . .'

Alice had almost looked forward to the journey then. She wanted to work hard and show what she could do. Perhaps it might even be beautiful over there in the east? And she was sure to find lots of other children to play with. At last she would be able to run and jump again. Alice had rushed through the straw in the hall and turned a cartwheel, so that her dress fell over her head. The guard had looked quite amazed.

Secretly, she had hoped that in this east, however big it turned out to be, she would see her parents again. As Daddy had so often said, 'Everything's possible'.

Towards morning, when they were driven out of the hall, Alice had asked a final question: 'But why is it only Jews who have to go to the east?'

And Grandfather had come up with an answer even then: 'People of the same kind generally get on better together. That's why. In any case, Jews are well known for being hard-working.'

Once again her eyes moved to Paul at the grating. In spite of his curls, he looked nothing like the man who had come to get them. Only very special people could have beautiful brown curls like Paul's.

Less than a day had passed since then, since their departure in the middle of the night. Now, looking back at it, she had so many questions. But Grandfather was still asleep and she did not want to disturb him.

6

•••

'Want to play?' asked David. 'We've got a pack of cards.'

Did she want to! She unbuttoned the two top buttons of her dress because by now it was very hot in the truck. David asked Ruth if he could have something to drink, but she said no, they had to economize on drinks. There was no way of knowing when they would get water.

Ruben shuffled and dealt the cards. Rebekka played too, and one of the many Maibaums, with whom Ruben had made friends. His name was Walter and they were about the same age.

You had to hold the cards close to your eyes to make out anything. It was an old, well-worn pack which showed nothing but faces: poets, composers, painters, actors, singers, directors, sculptors, architects – four from each profession. Alice was familiar with many of the names and she even recognized a few faces.

'I was given this game for my twelfth birthday,' Ruth announced.

'I shall be twelve in two months time,' said Alice proudly.

'I would have thought you were ten,' said Ruth.

Then they played and forgot everything: the heat, the stench, Struppi the dog, the screaming woman in the next truck, the bolted sliding-door and all the uncertainty to which they were travelling.

'Ruben, I want from you Red Two, Friedrich Schiller. Thanks. And have you also got Red Four, Heinrich Heine?'

Ruben had that card too and had to hand it over. Alice was triumphant, but when it was Rebekka's turn she relieved Alice of Franz Schubert and Jacques Offenbach, two cards of which Alice was very fond, because she knew the names well. Mummy and Daddy had often gone to concerts and had talked a lot about music, and long ago Mummy had also often played Offenbach on the piano.

'Heine and Offenbach,' said the trench-coat man to Ruth, his voice full of reproach. 'Better to get rid of a game like that . . .'

'It won't do any harm here,' said Ruth calmly.

Alice did not understand what they meant, but there was so much she did not understand. 'And you, Walter, have you got Green Three, Anselm Feuerbach?'

First Ruben won, then Rebekka, then Alice. When Walter won the next game, David flung down his cards and began to cry.

'It's only a game,' Ruth comforted him.

'But Struppi . . .' David sobbed.

Then Rebekka started crying too. Alice crawled over to her and put her arms round her. It comforted her too to feel her body and smell her skin. She stroked her face, her hair and hands, and was happy when Rebekka embraced her back. But then all of a sudden everything else came back – the stench, the heat, the dying dog, the screaming woman – and Alice became painfully aware that her parents were not there to comfort her. Perhaps she might not meet them in the east after all, and perhaps Grandmother would not come on the next train.

Alice's tears dripped on to Rebekka's yellow blouse, leaving spots.

'Be my friend,' whispered Alice.

'You're only eleven,' said Rebekka, letting her go. 'You simply have no idea.'

'Then tell me what I ought to know,' whispered Alice. 'I haven't learned anything for so long. I want to know *everything*.'

'Come here, child.' Grandfather's voice sounded vigorous and Alice turned. He pointed to the holdall. That meant he wanted her to sit beside him. She obeyed reluctantly. Grandfather took her hand in his own, then his head drooped and he nodded off again. Now she could not move from the spot without waking him up.

Two young men were standing in front of the second grating, talking to each other in low voices. One had a dark moustache, the other had his hair combed straight back and fixed with hair cream. His name was Max.

Now the sun was falling through the grating diagonally from above. For a moment the Persian lady's gold tooth flashed and Alice stared, fascinated. But then the woman shut her mouth. She got up and made her way over to Ruth. Alice heard her asking Ruth to hold up a coat in front of her. Ruth took Rebekka with her. The Persian coat was big and heavy, but they held it as wide open as they could. And they had to stand there a long time, so long that one or two people had actually begun to snigger. But Ruth gave them an angry look and they fell silent.

At last the woman reappeared from behind the coat. She thanked Ruth and Rebekka, her face red. She folded her coat carefully and sat on it.

Alice looked longingly across at Rebekka. Yes, she wanted

to learn everything, to catch up on everything. For two years she had lived in the tiny servants' flat in the basement. No one ever came to visit them and they visited no one. Only Mrs Lohmann had looked in every day, brought them food, taken up the rubbish, and from time to time she had had a little surprise for Alice: a book or some coloured crayons or home-made sweets. That meant a celebration every time, especially if it was a book. Her parents and grandparents had brought so few books down to the basement from the two upper floors.

Of course, all four adults had taken the most loving care of her. They had told jolly stories and even given her proper school lessons. And to Alice's great delight they had taught her draughts, Nine Men's Morris and chess. How many chess games had she played with Grandfather – all afternoon! And Grandmother had crocheted and knitted with her.

All the same, she had become very quiet, especially since her parents had gone away. Sometimes she had spent the whole day by the window. If she looked diagonally upwards through the panes, she could see a few breeze-blown twigs and a narrow patch of sky. The windows were half below ground level, each in a concrete well. Many years ago, Grandfather had built a little wall round the well, the height of a railing. In those days Daddy had been a small boy who was always playing on the paved area behind the house and without the wall he could easily have fallen into one of the wells.

Alice had sat for hours beside the windows, dreaming. She had yearned to be on the other side of the wall, to tear around the garden, or sit on the swing. Often she would have been happy if only a face had looked over the wall.

Sometimes a bird had alighted on it and sat there for a while, wagging its head to and fro, before flying away again. Those had been good moments for Alice.

The window-gazing time had not really begun until

Mummy and Daddy left. Six months ago Grandmother and Grandfather were still trying to entice her away from the window: Grandfather had done floor exercises with her and Grandmother had taught her cooking. But soon that was no longer interesting and she had gone back to the window. In the end, it could actually happen that Grandmother would call, 'Have a look out, Mousie. The clouds look so beautiful today!' and sometimes Grandfather had signalled to her, his finger to his lips, when there was a bird on the wall.

Once, when the bedroom window was open to air the place, in the surge of fresh air Alice had started shouting, just for the joy of it. Grandmother had hastily shut the window and Grandfather had put his hand over her mouth. Immediately afterwards, Mrs Lohmann had come downstairs: for God's sake, the child must not shout like that; she'd end up in the devil's kitchen!

In the middle of the truck sat a father with two sons. The father, a skinny man with a full black beard and a black hat on his head, was sitting cross-legged on the floor, reading a book. He sat bent double, with the book close to his eyes. The elder son, about seventeen years old, sat behind his father on a rucksack, leaning over his shoulder and reading with him. The younger son, an attractive black-eyed boy of thirteen or fourteen, was practising headstands on a pile of luggage. Very slowly, his legs bent, he shifted his body-weight to his head, balancing with outstretched arms. He took the greatest possible care not to disturb any of the people sitting round the luggage, but he did knock his father's hat off twice. His father calmly put it on again each time, after blowing the dust off it, and went on reading.

Headstands. She had practised them in the basement as well, but then her skirt would fall over her head and

Grandmother would say, 'Don't do that, Mousie. It's not proper for a girl.'

But secretly she had gone on trying, in the evening after bedtime, when Grandmother and Grandfather had turned off the light in the bedroom and gone back to the kitchen, where they slept on the pull-out sofa in the dining corner. Only in the darkness she had often got so giddy that she no longer knew which was up and which was down.

No, she would never be able to do a headstand as well as that Aaron Ehrlich. Every time her feet were almost up, fear of her own courage overcame her. But she had been the best in the class at cartwheels. Sometimes, when she was alone in the bedroom, she had actually practised cartwheels in the basement. She could manage exactly one cartwheel from wall to wall.

'Chemnitz!' cried Paul.

One or two people got up, crowded round the gratings and shouted for water, but there was room for no more than two heads at each grating.

'There will be water soon now,' Alice heard Mrs Maibaum tell her children.

'Chemnitz,' said Mr Blum to a man sitting beside him with his wife and three young daughters. He said it the way Grandfather said 'Delicious!' when he particularly liked something that Grandmother had cooked. 'I lived here for a long time.'

The wheels rattled over the points. Alice heard other engines whistling, other trains puffing. Their train was travelling more slowly now; it came to a stop, jerked forward again and began to move backwards.

'Are we going home again?' asked David in surprise.

But the train was only shunting. Then it moved on. For a while a breathless silence had filled the truck, but now people began to make a noise, some crying, others cursing.

'Pigs!' cried the young man with the moustache.

7

Just as her eyes closed again and a crescent moon grew and grew, cool and milky, in front of her, she heard someone groaning. The sound came from the corner where the pregnant woman was sitting. Alice craned forward cautiously, trying to see between the people. Her hand was still in Grandfather's. Yes, the thin, pale woman was the one who was groaning. A bald man wearing steel-rimmed glasses was bending over her. Alice was sure that he was the young woman's father, but where was her husband?

Ruth got up and went over to her, followed by Mr Blum. They leaned down and talked to her.

'Grandfather,' said Alice, 'why is she groaning like that?'

But Grandfather was snoring, his chin on his chest.

'She's going to have a baby,' said Rebekka.

Alice looked at her uncertainly. 'Do you mean her child will see the light of the world here in this truck?'

Rebekka grinned. 'Why do you talk so swankily? Nobody talks like that!'

'Mummy did,' said Alice shyly.

'Oh, for heaven's sake,' sighed Rebekka, with a sideways

glance at Alice's grandfather. 'I suppose you don't know anything about anything?'

David and Ruben giggled. Alice lowered her eyes. No, she didn't know anything, or at least not exactly. Once she had asked Grandmother how children came into the world. She had wanted to know exactly. It had been only a few weeks ago, but Grandmother had waved her aside: 'Later, child, later . . .'

'The baby comes out between her legs,' said Ruben.

'We have watched Struppi twice,' said David, his nose in the air.

Ruben put his arm round him.

Alice kept her eyes lowered but Rebekka scrambled across, sat down beside her and began to explain. She spoke very softly, always keeping an eye on Alice's grandfather. Once or twice Alice had to ask her to repeat something because the *rat-tat-tat* of the wheels and Grandfather's snores made it difficult to hear. But even then much of what she heard was not really clear to her. Rebekka repeated it patiently. Only when Ruben tried to join in, she went for him; he was to hold his tongue. And Alice learned everything: not only how the baby leaves the womb but also how it gets there.

Now the pregnant woman was standing up, leaning against the wall. She had both hands pressed to her stomach and was rocking herself to and fro.

'Where is her husband?' asked Alice.

'Over there, the one with the glasses,' said Rebekka.

Alice was amazed. How could a man as old as that be her husband?

'I know them,' said Rebekka. 'They are called Willi and Sarah Wormser. They lived not far from us. Believe me, they love each other. Very much, in fact. And that's the point, isn't it?'

Alice could not take her eyes off the woman.

'Don't stare like that,' said Rebekka. 'It's no pleasure to Sarah. In any case, you can't stare for as long as it will take her. It's her first, so it may take a long time.'

'What on earth will they put as place of birth on its birth certificate if it's born here in the truck?' said Ruben. 'Where we are at that moment, or where we've come from, or where we're going to?'

But no one answered. Then a dragging sound joined the *rat-tat-tat* of the wheels. The train slowed down and came to a halt. Again everyone crowded at the gratings. Even at the pee gap a man – the one with the black hat – pressed his face against the metal frame. Alice took her hand from her grandfather's, turned and spied through the knothole.

'What can you see?' asked Rebekka.

Alice saw a river valley with a gentle line of hills in the background. A narrow country road ran between river and railway line. A buzzard circled, while three big birds landed in the reeds. The water glittered. A beautiful picture in a round frame.

She let Rebekka look out, and then Ruben and David.

'Is it a station?' someone asked. But the section they could see through the knothole was too small to be sure. Nor could anything much clearer be seen through the gratings.

'If it is, it's a very small one,' said Mr Blum. 'You can't see any houses.'

David reported that guards were walking up and down the embankment again, and sure enough, if you put your ear to the wall, in spite of the noise inside the truck, you could hear the boots crunching on the gravel. And a man's voice too, a man clearing his throat.

'Guard,' called Mr Blum, 'there's a woman in labour in here!'

'Water!' cried Mrs Maibaum. 'We've got small children here. We need water.'

The blonde woman put her baby on Mrs Herz's lap and climbed over seated people and luggage to the sliding-door by which Alice was sitting. She took off one shoe and banged it on the door. 'Water!' she shouted as well, joined by Mrs Herz and Mr Blum, Paul and Ruth.

'You shout too, children!' cried Ruth.

The loudest was a bull-necked man crouching beside Alice. There was a big case between him and her. The woman beside him shouted too, her red cheeks turning even redder, and the bull-necked man's face turned as red as a lobster.

Many people began to shout in the neighbouring trucks as well, but after a time the shouts died down. One voice after another fell silent. Even from next door only a single voice could still be heard, crying softly, 'Lia, my little Lia . . .'

Outside nothing happened. Alice spied through the knot hole and saw the guard, the young one whom she already knew. The blonde returned, weeping, to her place.

'There is so much water outside,' said Paul, who was at the grating. 'They would only need to open the doors.' And he shouted out through the bars, 'I say, Mr Guard, open the door for us for just a minute. We will get water for ourselves.'

'The pregnant woman needs a doctor,' shouted Mr Blum.

But the guard was deaf to their shouts. He brushed away the beads of sweat running down his cheeks with the back of his hand, but his cheeks were just as wet a moment later.

The train did not stop for long but it became painfully hot in the truck. There was no longer the draught of their movement, and outside there was not a breath of air. The stink from the corner was revolting. The people sitting near it began to leave their places and move in among the others. The truck became hotter and more crowded.

'Grandfather, wake up.'

For a moment he seemed not to know where he was. He looked about him with an empty, almost idiotic expression. There was sweat on his forehead and upper lip. He took off his jacket and put it over his knees.

Alice too pulled off her shoes and stockings, but when she put her bare feet on the floor she suddenly cringed. This was where she had been sick; this was where David had trodden with his filthy shoe; this was where old dirt was still stuck in every crack. Perhaps on an earlier transport the lavatory muck heap had been just where she was sitting now. She hastily put on her shoes again and looked around. She must think about something else, anything rather than puke again!

Alice had only thought the word, not spoken it, and yet she went cold. She had heard it from Trudi, but when she had once used it at home everyone had been shocked. She had had to promise never, never to let it pass her lips again.

Paul, in his torn shirt, crouched under the grating beside the blonde woman and dozed. Other men and boys who had still been wearing their jackets a short while ago were now sitting in their shirt sleeves or vests, and the bull-necked man even had a bare torso. Alice was astonished to see his thick, dark chest hair, like a pelt. Grandfather had hair on his chest too, but not nearly as much.

Now the truck smelled not only of the muck heap but more and more penetratingly of sweat. Everyone was searching in their luggage, and field flasks and Thermoses appeared. Alice was thirsty too. Grandfather got her to stand up and took a bottle of fruit juice out of their holdall.

'Drink from the bottle,' he said. 'We can't afford to lose a single drop in the mug.'

Alice was amazed: no one in the family had ever drunk out of the bottle. 'Builders and coachmen drink out of the bottle,' Grandmother had said once.

She raised the bottle to her mouth and drank. The air that went back into the bottle after every swallow produced a whole series of little popping noises. That was fun, and the juice tasted wonderful. It was, after all, their good old elderberry juice. The cook had pressed it and thickened it from berries in their garden, in the old days when they had still lived on the two upper floors of the house and had a cook. Mummy had opened this bottle only on very special occasions, but during the last two years, the basement years, there had been no occasions.

They had had to economize so strictly on food – especially when Mummy and Daddy were still there. For some mysterious reason, which Grandfather also connected with the war, none of the Dubskys had gone shopping during the basement years. Everything they ate had been brought to the basement by Mrs Lohmann: bread, potatoes, vegetables and now and then a glass of clarified butter – and swedes, again and again. Fortunately, Mrs Lohmann's brother had a farm and although he was now a soldier, his wife brought food to Mrs Lohmann once a week in a rattle-trap of a delivery van, and Mrs Lohmann shared it with the Dubskys. Every time she brought food to the cellar for them, Grandfather and Daddy bowed to her, took the basket, bags or sack from her and thanked her warmly – though even so, they often did not really have enough to eat.

It seemed to Alice very odd that they never went up to visit Mrs Lohmann in the flat, and once, when Mrs Lohmann had had a visit from her sister-in-law, she did not come down to the basement at all.

And another odd thing: Alice had never been able to leave the house. Once, when she almost couldn't bear it any longer in the basement, she had pleaded with the grown-ups to let her go out, but they would not allow it.

'It's so dirty out in the streets now,' her grandmother had

told her nervously. 'You simply can't imagine. You could catch your death in that dirt.'

'What about Mrs Lohmann?' Alice asked.

'She's more robust than we are,' Grandfather had said hastily, and Grandmother had nodded, looking relieved.

At that time Mummy and Daddy had still been at home, but soon afterwards they had gone out twice together in the evening and then, suddenly, they had gone away.

Alice sighed. It was so hot. Her hair was quite straggly. Grandmother hated what she called rat-tails. As she always said, 'Anyone who doesn't look after their hair deserves to be bald.' She had taught Alice to brush her hair carefully every morning for a quarter of an hour or longer, but that night, before they left, she had had no time. Not even time to clean her teeth! For the first time on this journey, she looked at her watch: a quarter to two. Lunchtime.

8

'Here, you have some too,' said Alice, handing Rebekka the bottle.

Rebekka drank and passed the bottle on to David, who swallowed a little and handed it to Ruben. When the bottle came back to Grandfather, it was only half full. He took some juice in his mouth quite solemnly and kept it there for a long time, before swallowing it down in tiny portions, his eyes closed. Only several minutes after the last swallow did he open them again and say dreamily, 'Grandmother picked those berries . . .'

Alice leaned against him and whispered, 'Where do you think she is now?'

Grandfather shrugged his shoulders.

'In any case, she knows we're thinking about her,' said Alice.

'Would you like something to eat now?' asked Grandfather in a dull voice.

She shook her head. Before, when Grandfather was asleep, she had been hungry, but now she was feeling sick again.

There was a disturbance in the lavatory corner. An old

man was taking a very long time. His wife, who was holding a cross-stitched tablecloth in front of him, began to cry when some of the others grumbled and nagged. 'Oh, please, be kind to him . . .'

'Those are the Cohns,' Rebekka whispered to Alice. 'He used to be a teacher. And over there, the three dry old sticks with the fatty, they are the Herschel family.'

'What in all the world,' cried the red-cheeked woman to the weeping one, 'made you bring a tablecloth with you?'

The old woman looked at her uncertainly. 'You never know,' she said at last. 'Perhaps where we're going we shall have a new home. Then where are you without a tablecloth if guests come?'

The young woman laughed, but no one else laughed with her.

The old woman reminded Alice of Grandmother. Perhaps she was in a hospital bed now. Or perhaps she had been back in the basement for some time, doing her knitting.

Only, after all that had happened, would Grandmother be able to knit at all? She had never been alone before, and now she might be sitting alone in front of a plate of soup, moving restlessly between the kitchen and the sitting-room, or standing by the window, looking out. Alice felt a lump in her throat.

When they were taken away, there had been no dirt in the streets. They had been as clean as Alice remembered them. Had Grandmother been deceiving her? And why had Mummy and Daddy not told her the truth?

She pulled out the locket that she wore on a thin gold chain round her neck and opened it. There were Daddy and Mummy in a tiny photograph. Mummy was holding Alice in one arm – she must have been about as old then as the blonde woman's little curly-head. Mummy had given her the locket for her last birthday, the eleventh. Alice loved it because it was so old and because there were so many memories attached to it. Mummy had been given it on her own fifteenth birthday by her parents, with a photograph of them, and she had always preserved it like a treasure, although she owned much more expensive jewellery. Mummy's parents had been dead for a long time.

She also had three letters with her, sent to her by Mummy and Daddy since they left. They had become quite grey and tattered from being pressed so often to her lips. She had snatched them from under her mattress at the very last minute and pushed them into her coat pocket.

Grandmother and Grandfather had assured her that her parents were doing well where they were now. They had telephoned Mrs Lohmann several times and sent their love. Alice wondered why they did not write. Then came her first letter, followed at almost equal intervals by two more: brief, typed letters in which Mummy and Daddy told her how very much they were looking forward to seeing her again soon. And she was to be good with Grandmother and Grandfather and not always asking to go out. And much love from Mummy and Daddy.

Alice could repeat them by heart, all three letters. The only extraordinary thing was that where they were now, Mummy and Daddy had a typewriter in which the capital D stuck just like the one on Grandfather's old typewriter. When she pointed this out to him, he had been quite speechless for a moment and then he had said that that really was a quite extraordinary coincidence. And how observant she was!

'Where, Madam? To the east, everyone to the east,' the fat man had said. In that case it really was quite possible that she would find Mummy and Daddy where she was being sent now. The east could surely not be so huge that the Dubsky couple would be impossible to find. And if they were writing their letters on a typewriter, things could not be going all that badly for them.

'What are you thinking about, Mousie?' asked Grandfather. His good white shirt was sticking to his body. He gave her a tired smile.

'You know,' she replied, smiling back.

'I wish everything were still as it was six months ago,' he sighed. 'I would be quite content with that – the five of us in our basement.'

'No,' she said, 'I don't want to go back to the basement, ever.'

'You don't know what you're saying, Alice,' he said.

She listened intently. For the first time she could remember, he had called her Alice. Was it because she had contradicted him quite seriously?

She sensed an uncomfortable feeling in her stomach, a feeling of tightness, not of sickness. Over in the corner Max, the hair-cream man, was squatting, with no coat, no cross-stitched cloth held in front of him.

No one even glanced at him; they were used to the sight by now. Only Mrs Herz was staring in his direction, although the blonde, curly-haired toddler on her lap was tugging at her hair and crowing, 'Look at me! Me!'

Ruth was back in her place and Rebekka leaned against her, as if she had not seen her for days. Both of them dozed off. Even the pregnant woman was asleep now in her corner.

Alice could see a long way down Rebekka's blouse. Had Rebekka already got breasts?

Perhaps the feeling in her stomach came from the stench. She turned round and pressed her nose against the knothole, but nothing but heat came in. The tight feeling increased and her insides began to rumble. She peered out through the knothole: the river was glittering seductively, children were bathing from the banks, a boy bicycling along the country road stopped and gaped at the train. A guard yelled at him,

'Get a move on, lad! Nothing to gape at here. I'll get you going!' The boy pedalled fearfully away.

Now she could hear David in the truck, shouting with delight. Alice turned. Paul was letting David look through the grating, and every time he tried to put him down, David began to kick and say, 'Again, Paul, again!' until the young man put him on the floor and said, 'No more now. Enough!'

Paul was never left in peace. He was gleaming with sweat. The small children in the truck all flew towards him, demanding one after another to be lifted up to the grating. Then, when each had seen enough, they made Paul do a puppet show with his hands. One hand was Punch, the other the devil. Of course, the devil was trying to make a fool of Punch, but however cunningly he tried, Punch was always the winner.

Even Grandfather looked on with interest, clapped, and was not irritated when the children walked on his feet.

But at the moment when Alice was going to tell him about her stomach pains, he got up painfully and made his way to the pee crack. Alice hunched her shoulders and did not dare to look. In the past, on walks, he had always gone a long way off to pee and if Alice had run after him, he had sent her firmly away.

Alice's insides were churning. Could it be the elderberry juice? She was doubled up with pain, sweat bursting from every pore.

'Grandfather,' she moaned.

He turned, startled.

'Grandfather!'

He pushed his way hurriedly through the seated people. She had jumped up and was moving towards him.

'Grandfather, I . . .'

'Wait,' he said. 'I'll get my coat.'

'Not here!' she sobbed. 'I want to go out!'

She threw a fearful glance at the corner. The heap was breaking up, flowing outward in tongues, like slowly cooling liquid lava. She had seen a picture of it in one of Grandfather's books. It looked like a great, live animal, threatening the people.

'Mousie,' said Grandfather, stroking her hair.

'I'm so ashamed . . .'

In a great hurry he took a roll of lavatory paper from her own rucksack, picked up his coat and returned to her as quickly as he could. She was holding her stomach and crying.

'Don't think. Clench your teeth,' said Grandfather. 'A German girl is not afraid.'

At that Ruth opened her eyes and cried sharply, '*What* did you say? Are you mad, man?'

9

•••

Alice had to go three times in succession. Diarrhoea. There was a queue waiting in front of the corner. When she had got rid of everything in the end, she lay on Grandfather's lap, completely exhausted. Grandfather was sitting on the coat and the holdall. Alice wept with shame; it was all so disgusting. Grandfather talked to her softly, but she did not hear what he was saying.

The train was still standing in the afternoon sun.

'This is murder!' shouted a man's voice from the neighbouring truck.

Alice's eyes opened with shock.

'And God lets it happen!' screamed a woman. 'What have we done? Just lived our lives like everyone else!'

'Those people outside see the trains passing and no one does anything!'

'Afterwards they will say they didn't know anything about it,' moaned the woman. 'Saw nothing, heard nothing.'

'They are animals,' said the man with the big moustache. 'Beasts. It's a shame such people should inhabit the earth . . .'

'You talk about them the way they talk about us,' said Paul, and stopped doing his Punch performance.

'Who are they talking about?' whispered Alice.

'No idea,' said Grandfather.

'I know exactly,' said Ruth. 'They are talking about the Germans.'

'Aren't we German?' asked Alice, surprised.

'You used to live in Germany, that's all,' said Ruth. 'Jews who once lived in Germany.'

'Please,' said Grandfather, almost begging.

There was silence in the truck. Many people were asleep, others dozing. From time to time paper rustled or mugs clinked. The baby grizzled; the curly-haired toddler and the youngest Maibaum boy whined in a monotonous sing-song. Now all four Maibaum children were naked down to the underpants.

Alice noticed the red-cheeked young woman beside the bull-necked man. She too had closed her eyes. Her head was on his lap, his hand inside her blouse.

Grandfather looked in the same direction and his expression darkened. 'Aren't they ashamed?' he hissed.

But Bull-neck kept his hand in the woman's blouse. 'Old fool!' was all he said.

The woman laughed, took his face between her hands and kissed him passionately. Grandfather turned Alice away so that she was forced to look in the opposite direction, where Paul had given in to the children and was performing again.

'Hey,' said Punch to the devil, 'you went and stopped the engine, didn't you, and I bet you don't know how to get it going again, you idiot!'

The children laughed. The devil pretended to be offended and tried to show that he knew all about engines. *Whoosh*, he disappeared.

'Big mouth!' Punch shouted after him. 'We'll just see how long you take. I'll have a kip in the meantime!'

He too disappeared, and now Paul's hands became the robber and the princess. He was strong but stupid; she was weak but clever. He wanted to carry her off and she kept on distracting him. How foolish he was! He couldn't even read and write. The children screeched with pleasure. The most abandoned were the two little girls with the hair ribbons. The elder was probably already going to school; the younger might have been four. Alice laughed too.

'Children laughing, in a cattle truck full of shit . . .'

Alice choked. The person who had said that was Grandfather.

'What?' she asked, dumbfounded.

'It just slipped out,' said Grandfather, embarrassed. 'Sorry!'

Alice stared at him as if at a stranger. If the word had just slipped out, it must have been inside him to begin with.

As a little girl she had once walked with Grandmother past a drunk. He had kept on shouting out that word, dribbling and waving his arms about. Her grandmother had told her very seriously and emphatically that only vulgar people ever said such a word. Over and over, later on too, Grandmother had talked about 'vulgar people', pulling down the corners of her mouth scornfully as she spoke.

So was Grandfather vulgar too? Impossible. All the same, he had used the word 'shit'. Might he also be capable of waving his arms about and dribbling?

She lay very still, thinking. Then she heard his stomach rumbling.

'Alice,' he said dully. 'Sweetheart, I think I've got it too . . .' He pressed his hand against his stomach.

She looked at him in dismay.

'There's no way out of it,' he sighed.

'But I can't hold your coat up so high, Grandfather,' she whimpered. 'It's so heavy and you're so tall!'

Paul pushed the children aside and asked if he could help.

'It's nothing,' said Grandfather, but Alice picked up the coat and gestured with her chin towards the corner. Paul nodded and understood. They held the coat together, at a right angle; not even Alice herself could see her grandfather. In any case, she was far too busy trying not to tread on the stinking mush.

'We are sure to be next,' said Rebekka. 'It was the juice . . .'

Alice helped Grandfather back to the holdall. He was so exhausted that he did not try to stop her when she folded up his coat on the floor and sat on it. Change of seat, that was all. Now, when she looked up at him, he stood out like a monument. His hands were shaking and there was sweat on his forehead. He was staring into space.

'Grandfather,' Alice whispered, 'don't you feel well?'

Then he tipped to one side. Jumping up, she clasped him and pushed her whole weight against him.

'Grandfather!' she screamed.

Ruth and Paul came to her aid at the same moment, taking the heavy body from her and setting him upright again. Ruth fetched the damp cloth on which David and his family had wiped their fingers and put it on Grandfather's forehead. Its coolness seemed to do him good. He opened his eyes and his colour began to return. Paul fanned him. From all sides advice was fired at Ruth, and together with Paul, they moved the holdall a little further from the wall so that Grandfather could lean back more comfortably.

'There, now you've got your grandfather back again,' said Ruth.

Alice gave Ruth and Paul a grateful smile and crouched down again on the coat. Now she was responsible for him. She thought about it as she sat holding his hand. Was the holdall soft enough for him? But he had her coat underneath him as well. And the bag under it yielded quite a bit. 'Would you like something to eat or drink, Grandfather?'

No, he did not want anything. He wanted only to rest, so she sat quite still where she was. It was uncomfortable holding his hand and her arm grew numb, but when she tried cautiously to withdraw her hand she felt the energy with which Grandfather squeezed it, so she went on sitting.

Alice thought about her parents. Her longing for them was so great that it hurt. How was she to manage with Grandfather, when he was no longer the big, strong protector? Twisting her body with difficulty, without letting go of his hand, she fished the three letters out of her coat pocket. She took the last letter and unfolded it with her left hand and her lips. Although she knew it by heart, she read it:

Dear Mousie,
We hope you got our first two letters. We can't write from here as regularly as we would like, but don't worry about us. We're doing well here. Mummy's dental treatment will not last very much longer. We are already looking forward so much to being with you again afterwards. We know we don't have to worry about you either. You will have the best possible care with Grandmother and Grandfather. Always be obedient and make them happy. You can always rely on what they say and do.

We think of you every day. We talk and dream of you and can hardly wait for the moment that will bring us all together again.

All our love,
Mummy and Daddy

She kissed the place where *Mummy and Daddy* was written, folded the letter again and put it back in her coat pocket with the other two.

Together. Yes. Perhaps very soon. She took a deep breath.

'Who has anything left to drink?' asked the trench-coat man. 'I'll buy it off them.'

No one answered. The children had gone back to their mothers and fallen asleep. David and Ruben were sleeping too. The three skinny Herschel sisters and their fat brother seemed to have melted into a single lump. And now, in the silence, they could hear the rushing of the river and the hum of insects.

The whole truck had filled up with mosquitoes and horse-flies. They were buzzing particularly thickly round Grandfather's face.

Cautiously Alice withdrew her hand, stood up and tried to wave away the mosquitoes so that he could sleep peacefully. How old he looked. Really drawn and weak.

He started, slapped his cheek with his hand and opened his eyes. 'Mosquitoes,' he said sleepily. 'Did I doze for long, sweetheart?'

She did not know. It had seemed endlessly long to her, but when she looked at her watch she could see that the train had been standing there for only an hour.

'As long as we're not going forwards, there's a chance that we might go backwards some time,' said Grandfather.

No, thought Alice, but she said nothing. She did not want to hurt him.

'No stomach-aches, no griping pains,' said Ruth. 'It looks as if we've escaped.'

Alice knew how relieved she must be, and was grateful to Ruth for not blaming Grandfather for the juice.

10

•••

Alice saw Grandfather taking the elderberry juice bottle out of the holdall. Then he strode across the luggage and the curly-headed child to Paul's grating and pushed the bottle through the bars. It was only then that Alice realized what he was doing.

'Don't!' cried Paul. 'In the spot we're in we could . . .'

'Undiluted elderberry juice,' said Grandfather. 'You saw the results.'

'We're going to get water some time!' cried Paul.

But then the bottle broke on the gravel of the embankment, with such a crash that the sleepers in the truck started up.

'Shits!' a guard cursed outside the truck.

'Pity I didn't hit him,' growled Grandfather, returning to his place.

Alice stared at him, but he avoided her eyes. Obviously he was feeling strong enough now to sit on the floor himself while Alice had the holdall, but she refused firmly and pushed him back on the holdall. It was nothing to her to sit doubled up, and besides, it was easier to squirm between Ruth's children to Rebekka.

Rebekka was asleep. She had sunk backwards on to a bag in the midst of the Maibaum family.

None of them was bothered, neither parents nor grandparents, nor the six children who were now asleep, snuggled together: two grown-up daughters, three school-age sons and a little one who had been staggering around on bow legs, dragging his nappy behind him. The little boys had snotty noses and the Maibaums' clothes looked grubby. Alice could well imagine that her grandmother would have forbidden her to have anything to do with them.

A little way off, the Grün girls with the ribbons in their hair were quarrelling. They wanted something to drink. Mr Grün went on writing on his knees and the children tugged and pulled at his trouser legs. He scolded them quietly.

Alice was also terribly thirsty now. She swallowed with a dry mouth.

'Grandfather,' she whispered, 'have we anything more to drink?'

'Coffee,' he said. 'A Thermos full of coffee. I hope it's still warm.'

'What for?' she asked. 'It's so hot already, and Grandmother always said that coffee was not for children.'

Without answering, Grandfather took the Thermos out of the rucksack, filled the screw-on top, tasted it and pulled a face. But he took another gulp.

'Lukewarm,' he said, 'nasty.'

He handed the top to Alice, who drank it all and then put the Thermos away. The thick, black drink really did taste horrible, but it smelled just the same as it had always smelled in their basement.

Mrs Wormser, the pregnant woman, had begun to groan again. She must be in great pain.

Grandmother had not made that coffee on the night they were taken away. The uniformed men would not have given her enough time. She had made it and filled the Thermos the night before, as she had done every evening since they'd lived in the basement. And every morning she had poured coffee from the Thermos into their cups.

Grandfather had always been in charge of grinding the coffee. Alice heard again the quiet squeaking of the coffee mill and smelled the fragrance of the freshly ground coffee beans. She knew about the two big boxes under the bed. Originally they had been full of packets of coffee, but bit by bit they had emptied. Mrs Lohmann also had her share.

'At least it's a way of showing our appreciation,' Grandfather had said.

Sometimes Mrs Lohmann had been nervous. How could any house smell so strongly of coffee in the middle of a war? It was suspicious. But Grandfather had calmed her down. She had only to point out that the house had previously belonged to a coffee wholesaler and that strong smells lasted for years in the walls. After Grandmother had given her a little packet of coffee, Mrs Lohmann would go upstairs again, reassured. Real coffee beans had become so rare since the war had begun.

On Mummy's dental visits, not long before they left, coffee had also been discussed. About six months ago, Mummy suddenly had dreadful toothache and simply lay rolled up on her bed, whimpering. Her face was swollen, and even Grandmother's hot-water bottle had not helped.

When Mrs Lohmann came down, she and Daddy and Grandfather whispered together. Mrs Lohmann went away, and came back later with an address which she gave to Daddy. 'He's expecting you and your wife at eight o'clock, tonight,' she had told Daddy.

He had looked greatly relieved. This dentist had been a former class-mate of his, whom he often talked about. They had played football together; they had made experiments with Daddy's chemistry box and filled the house with horrible smells. 'He's a decent man,' he had told Mummy.

Now Alice was wide awake in spite of the heat. Her memory became as clear as glass. They had gone off in the darkness, Mummy taking three packets of coffee with her – 'So that we don't come empty-handed' – but Daddy had frowned and said, 'What he's doing for us can't be repaid with three bags of coffee.'

While her parents were away, Grandmother and Grandfather had kept on looking at each other and starting at every sound. Alice had been unable to understand their agitation. Mummy had gone to the dentist and Daddy had gone with her. What was so upsetting about that? And Grandfather's comment, which was apparently to reassure Grandmother, was completely incomprehensible to Alice, 'You would hardly know from their looks . . .'

But then Mummy and Daddy had come back safe and sound, and Alice's grandparents had been so noisy in their joy that Mrs Lohmann had knocked on the floor. Mrs Lohmann attached great importance to absolute quiet. Whenever Alice talked or laughed a little too loudly, she would hear Grandmother's everlasting, 'Ssh, ssh, Mrs Lohmann wants us to be quiet!'

But Mummy's tooth had calmed down for only three days before the pain became worse than ever and her face swelled up. Once again Mrs Lohmann and Daddy had whispered together, once again she had gone away and come back again: 'At eight-thirty.'

That was the evening when Alice saw her parents for the last time. The next morning their beds were empty. Alice had to stay in the bedroom. Grandmother was sobbing quietly in the kitchen. Alice heard Mrs Lohmann coming and going. Then Grandmother had come into the bedroom, red-eyed, and packed the holdall in hectic haste. 'What's going on?' Alice had asked again and again, but her only answer had been, 'Quiet, quiet!'

In all this extraordinary excitement, Grandmother had actually forgotten to give her her breakfast. Finally she had been allowed to come into the kitchen, but when Mrs Lohmann appeared, her face drawn, she had to go back to the bedroom. It had been a frightening day.

It had taken Grandfather and Grandmother a long time to calm down again. Days, weeks. And Mummy and Daddy had not come back. At first Alice had run to the door at every sound. Then Grandfather had explained it all to her: Mummy's tooth had been so septic that she had had to go off to a dental clinic, a long, long way away. Daddy had not wanted to let her go alone, so he had gone too.

'And why didn't they take me?' Alice asked.

'They don't want any healthy children in a dental clinic,' Grandfather told her. 'And your parents know there's nowhere you can be better cared for than with Grandmother and me.'

Alice would ask when they were coming back, but Grandfather could not give her a clear answer. 'Soon, Mousie, soon,' he always said. 'As soon as Mummy's tooth is really better.'

Of course. He could not know ahead of time when that would be, and as it turned out, the treatment went on and on. Sometimes she had asked Grandmother where the clinic was and Grandmother had said, 'I don't know exactly, Mousie. Ask Grandfather.'

And he had cleared his throat and answered, after a long pause. 'A long, long way to the east.'

But what was the meaning of Mrs Lohmann's whisper, which Alice had overheard through the bedroom door two days after Mummy's and Daddy's departure?

'In any case, it was *not* Dr Glossner,' she had said.

Alice had asked Grandfather about it afterwards, but he had waved his hand. 'She was talking about quite different people.' And he had added, his face stern, 'And in any case, you don't listen behind doors. That's not the way to behave, Mousie.'

A beam of afternoon sunlight shone in diagonally through the opposite grating, on the wall above the Herschels.

11

•••

Suddenly the woman in the Persian coat stood up. Her hair was untidy, her dress creased. She stretched out her arms and cried in a strong voice, 'I have sung at the greatest opera houses. Men have lain at my feet.' Then she laughed and said more quietly, 'And now this.'

Alice shrank back. What an ugly laugh the woman had. But it was easy to imagine that she had once been a famous singer. She was standing as if turned to stone, one arm raised, the other lowered, fingers outspread. Her head was bent and a little on one side. The seated people looked up at her, dazed with sleep.

'Do calm down,' sighed Mrs Maibaum. 'You must save your strength, even if you were the Empress of China.'

The singer went on standing silently in her pose, merely shaking her head almost imperceptibly.

'Sing!' cried Mr Blum. 'Sing something for us!'

Slowly the woman lifted her head and smiled. She put one hand on her breast and began to sing, first softly, then more loudly. Alice listened breathlessly. The song was about a trout swimming in a stream. The woman sang it in such a way that

Alice could see the fish playing in the clear water and feel the cool ripples.

Everyone listened intently, but when the singer had finished Alice heard the trench-coat man grumble, 'Can't even get a bit of sleep.'

But Alice clapped, and apart from the trench-coat man and his wife, everyone else clapped too.

'How beautifully you sing,' said Mrs Herz.

'But what's the use of water if it's only in a song?' said the blonde woman next to her. She snatched off her shoe again, banged it on the wall behind her and shouted, 'Water, water, water!'

The Maibaums, all ten of them, jumped up, their hands suddenly filled with shoes, spoons, pots and pans, and banging in time they too shouted, 'Wa-ter, wa-ter!'

Paul stamped his foot on the planks and joined in. The shouting grew louder and louder. Ruth and her children joined in the chorus, and so did Mr Ehrlich and his sons, and even Bull-neck and his girlfriend. All of them stamped their feet on the floor at the same time.

So did Alice.

But Grandfather just shook his head. Alice was annoyed with him. He had such a loud voice, why would he not join in?

There was noise coming from the other trucks too. Everyone was shouting for water.

'Pointless,' said Grandfather. 'Quite pointless.'

Alice peered through the knothole to see how the uniformed men were taking it, but in the little frame available there were no guards. On the other hand, a lot of children were now standing in the road, staring, and a horse-drawn wagon, piled high with hay, came to a stop. Four women and a man were sitting on the hay and they too were looking at the train. A bus driving by slowed down. Two bicyclists put on their brakes.

'Louder,' cried Alice, 'louder!'

But at that very moment the engine whistled and the shouting died away. Shortly afterwards there was a sudden jolt and the train set off. Alice, still at the knothole, saw a tiny station in open country as they passed.

'Must have been an unscheduled stop,' said the trench-coat man. 'If they had opened the doors here half the people would have run off. Those few men in the transport guard could not possibly have held everyone back.'

Grandfather nodded. The train was sure to stop soon at a proper station. There they would get water.

'You were wonderful,' Alice heard Ruth tell the singer.

Her song and the shouting had cheered the people in the truck. Max and the man with the moustache climbed over to Paul and started a whispered but lively conversation. Moustache gesticulated vigorously, Max simply listened, nodding from time to time. Mrs Herz tugged at his trousers from behind and murmured, 'Put something on, it's draughty.'

But Max brushed her hand away as if it were an irritating fly. Alice was surprised: how pale, how wretched he looked, and what had Mrs Herz to do with him? He was grown up, after all. Couldn't he look after himself?

Once Paul pointed to the sliding-door and Moustache turned his thumb down. Max nodded thoughtfully.

The brown pile in the corner had become a landscape with hills, plains and lakes. The trench-coat pair had to move still further away. Mrs Herz pulled her rucksack closer.

'What will happen?' she asked, 'if it goes on like this? In the end we're all going to be sitting right in the shit.'

David and Ruben moved over to the Maibaum children. Beside them a circle of older men had gathered, now joined by old Mr Cohn, moving stiffly. The father of the three young girls, who had up to now talked only to Mr Blum, was telling jokes.

'Imagine still being able to make jokes!' scolded the blonde woman.

'Oh, child,' sighed Mrs Herz. 'That Mr Silbermann – just let him keep talking.'

Rebekka, who already knew most of the jokes, moved towards Alice.

'Shall I plait your hair? Loose hair gets dirty so easily. Plaits are much more practical.'

And before Alice could answer, she felt a comb in her hair; Rebekka was bending over her, making a centre parting before starting to plait.

Alice had wanted plaits for a long time, like the girls at Uncle Ludwig and Aunt Irene's cattle yard, but Mummy and Grandmother could not bear plaits. Now she kept quite still, enjoying the prickly feeling on her scalp.

'I shall soon be too old for plaits,' said Rebekka. 'When I'm fifteen I'll be allowed to have my hair waved.' Then she asked Alice if she liked poetry.

Alice did not know what to say. There were of course many poetry books in Grandfather's bookcase, but she preferred stories. Her favourite story was Oscar Wilde's *The Nightingale and the Rose*. She had cried over that.

'Poems are nicer than stories,' said Rebekka. 'My favourite poem is by Mörike: *Orplid*. I know it by heart.' She stopped her plaiting and whispered in Alice's ear.

Alice did not quite understand the poem. Part of it was about a country by the sea, part about a child served by kings, but it sounded very beautiful. Alice closed her eyes, seeing a distant coastline shimmering in the sun.

'Too difficult for you,' said Rebekka, 'but I know another that I like very much too.'

The poem was called '*The Nix*' and was by August Kopisch. That really was a story. The nix, a water sprite, sang by a waterfall, playing its harp, and birds and trees listened, enchanted. But a pair of urchins shouted, 'Don't bother singing, you're not human, so you won't get to heaven.' The nix looked at the children, began to cry and sank into the water.

The waterfall roared angrily, the nightingale flew away, the trees shook. What were the urchins thinking of, to hurt the nix's feelings? They all cried, 'Come back, Nix! You sing so beautifully. Anyone who sings can go to heaven. Come back! The boys were only joking.'

So it rose out of the water again, struck a chord on its harp and began to sing, and everyone listened as before.

Alice fell under the spell of the story. The nix – so strange and different, probably green, with scales.

'And you?' she heard Rebekka ask. 'Don't you know any poems by heart?' Alice thought. She could scarcely offer Rebekka baby poems from the first and second classes. Then she remembered a very short poem which was on the gravestone of an eleven-year-old girl who had been Mummy's friend. She had drowned while bathing. In earlier days, when they had still lived in the upper floors of the house, Mummy had taken Alice to the cemetery from time to time to tend the graves of her parents, and each time they had visited that child's grave as well.

At first Mummy had read out the words to her, but later the knew it by heart. Of course she did not yet fully understand it, but it was beautiful and mysterious. And she whispered it to Rebekka: '*Take me, Oh Love, to thee – ever thy child to be, till the day dawns.*'

Rebekka nodded, and it was some time before she went on plaiting. 'Very short, but very beautiful,' she said. 'I shall make a note of that.' She repeated the three lines until she could say them fluently, and by then she had finished the plaits.

'Now you really do look nearly twelve,' she said, satisfied. Alice would have loved to see herself with her new hairstyle.

12

•••

Alice looked up at her grandfather, dozing with his eyes shut. What would he have to say about it?

'Mrs Lohmann gave me some beautiful hair ribbons,' she told Rebekka. 'She thought I ought to have plaits too, but I don't think Grandmother packed the ribbons. Pity.'

She saw that the ends of the plaits were already beginning to loosen.

'Have you got your periods yet?' whispered Rebekka.

Alice felt really stupid. Once again she had not understood.

'Oh, child, do you have to have *everything* explained to you?' groaned Rebekka. 'I'm getting sick of it.'

All the same, she explained what periods were, and Alice could not believe her ears. Was *that* going to happen to her too one day?

'Until you have your periods, you're still a child,' Rebekka whispered.

Everything went round and round in Alice's head. She could not sit beside Rebekka any longer. Turning back to

Grandfather, she pressed herself against him. He blinked and smiled at her. Then he sat up sharply and said, 'What *do* you look like?'

Alice hastily undid her plaits and ran her fingers through her hair until it hung on her shoulders as before. Grandfather put his arm round her and once again she felt quite safe.

She had had the same feeling on her last birthday. Her parents were still at home and Mrs Lohmann had picked a bunch of autumn flowers from the garden and made marzipan sweets, which Alice loved. Grandmother had given her a hand-knitted, coloured cap and matching scarf – although she was never allowed to go out. Grandfather had presented her with a particularly fat book from his bookcase, which she could scarcely lift, full of pictures of pyramids, temples, amphitheatres and churches, statues and famous paintings.

'You must keep looking at these, Mousie,' Grandfather had said, 'so that you know what man is capable of.'

Mummy had given her her own jewel box with all her jewellery in it. She had kept nothing for herself, not even the locket.

And after weeks of secrets, Daddy had given her a big roll of paper. On it he had painted Alice's family tree, from her great-great-grandparents down to her. He had decorated the name Alice Dubsky with beautiful curlicues. 'Without all of them there would be no you,' he had told her. 'And just remember that you must always behave so that you need never be ashamed in their presence.'

Alice had the cap and scarf in her rucksack, but the jewel box and the family tree must still be at home. If Grandmother had gone back to the basement flat, she would take care of these precious presents until the great reunion. And if she had to stay in hospital, Mrs Lohmann would guard her treasures.

Then she remembered that Mrs Lohmann had also had to

leave with them in the night. A shiver ran down Alice's back. What would become of her things if neither Grandmother nor Mrs Lohmann went home?

When Alice looked up she saw old Mrs Cohn squatting over in the corner. She was wearing a headscarf under which her white hair gleamed. Her husband was still crouching in his place. His eyes were closed and he looked quite exhausted. The cross-stitched tablecloth lay neatly folded on a case.

Alice got up, climbed over and picked up the cloth. When Mr Cohn tried to hold on to it, she pointed to his wife. She went to the corner, unfolded the cloth and held it up until Mrs Cohn had finished.

Then the three Silbermann girls came over to Rebekka from Mr Blum's side. They were rather chubby. The youngest had a thick plait down her back, the eldest had a perm. Both of them had protruding teeth, but the middle one, with the bobbed hair, was pretty and looked like her father.

Rebekka beckoned Alice, so she came and squashed in with the circle of girls. She discovered that the Silbermann girls were called Ida, Ilse and Isolde. They showered Alice with questions, wanting to know her name, her age and her previous address. 'Is that your grandfather?' and 'Can you play the piano?' They barely left her the time to answer their questions. Ida wanted to know if Alice and Rebekka found the lavatory corner as disgusting as she did, and Isolde was interested in Rebekka's father.

'My mother is divorced,' said Rebekka, frowning. 'My father is half-Jewish. He only got his head out of the noose by getting divorced.' She fell into a sombre silence.

'Our mother is half-Jewish too,' said Ilse, 'but she didn't get divorced. She stayed with us.'

'We'll get by just the same,' said Rebekka, still more sombrely.

The circle grew. The two Ehrlich sons had joined it now.

The elder was called Samuel. Alice looked at Aaron, the younger, with admiration. What dark eyes, what long, thick lashes he had!

'What about *your* parents?' asked Isolde, turning to Alice.

'Mummy has been in a dental clinic for six months,' Alice told them, 'and Daddy is with her.'

All the children stared at her.

'Aren't you Jewish?' asked Ida.

'Yes, I am,' said Alice, surprised. 'But what's that got to do with it?'

'If your parents are Jews,' said Samuel, 'then they're not in any dental clinic.' And he added, 'At least, not here in Germany.'

'They're in the east,' said Alice.

'Aha,' cried Ida and Ilse triumphantly.

'Did they have to leave very suddenly?' asked Isolde.

Alice nodded, bewildered.

'And they took next to nothing with them?' asked Samuel.

'No,' said Alice, 'of course not. They went straight from the dentist to the clinic.'

'And who told you all that?' asked Rebekka.

'Grandmother and Grandfather.'

'In a dental clinic!' said Ilse, shaking her head.

'Leave her alone,' said Aaron roughly.

Alice's head was spinning. She grasped Rebekka's arm.

'What do you mean?' snapped Isolde. 'She's going to find out anyway.' Turning to Alice, she said, 'You're too old for those fairy-stories.'

'Where are my parents, then, if they're not in a dental clinic?' asked Alice, her voice trembling.

Then the others talked about 'there'. You had to keep healthy, said Samuel, and be able to work. They needed strong workers. He put his arm round Isolde.

'What if you're too young to work?' asked Ida.

Samuel did not know. He guessed that children would stay with their mothers until they were big enough.

'And the old people?' asked Rebekka, glancing at Grandfather.

He shrugged his shoulders. 'Perhaps there's something like an old people's home or a hospital in the camp.'

'The camp?' asked Alice pitifully.

'A prison camp for us lot,' said Aaron. 'With barbed wire round it, and barracks, and guards.' He twisted his face into a sorrowful smile and added, 'But at least there's no school there.'

'You mean we're prisoners?' asked Alice, shocked.

'Man,' said Samuel, 'your people have left you absolutely clueless. Did they keep you in Rapunzel's tower?'

Alice felt as if she had been dowsed with cold water. Her head thumped and sang. As if from a distance, she heard Rebekka: 'That school business is bad. Who knows how long it's going to go on? We shall have missed so many years of school – and I want to be a doctor.'

'Architect, me,' said Samuel. He pointed to his brother. 'And he wants to be a cellist.'

'I can be that without school, anyway,' said Aaron loudly.

At that moment the pregnant woman began to groan again. Ruth climbed across to her and the circle broke up.

Alice returned in a daze to her grandfather, but instead of sitting down beside him she stood in front of him, staring at him. His eyes were shut, but under her gaze he opened them, smiled at Alice and reached for her hand. She pulled it away.

'There's a draught,' he said, shivering, and pulled his jacket across his chest.

She stared dumbly at him.

'I dreamed about Grandmother,' he said, in a shaking voice. 'She was happy and cheerful, like before . . .' He pulled out the linen handkerchief with which he had wiped the vomit from Alice's face, bent his head and blew his nose for a long time.

'I'm thirsty,' said Alice, her voice hard.

13

•••

The Thermos was in Alice's rucksack. Grandfather struggled with the laces, which were knotted. His hands were so big and awkward, and now they were shaking too, but Alice did not help him. When at last he had tugged the Thermos out of the rucksack, Alice took it from his hand and filled the top for herself.

'Not so much!' he cried.

But she drank it all without putting the top down. Then she wiped her mouth with the back of her hand and asked, 'Grandfather, where are Mummy and Daddy?'

He looked at her in surprise. 'But, child, you know . . .'

'In the east, yes,' she said. 'Somewhere in the east – in a camp, not a dental clinic. And they didn't go willingly. And we are prisoners too, being taken to a camp.'

With each phrase that she flung at him, Grandfather's head sank lower, and he sat bowed in silence.

'Because we are Jews!' she shouted. 'And you kept it all secret from me!'

There was silence in the truck.

'But, Mousie,' he groaned, 'how could we . . . You are still so young.'

'I shall never believe you again!' wailed Alice.

'You could not possibly have understood the truth,' said Grandfather almost inaudibly. '*We* scarcely understand it.'

'I would have understood,' cried Alice. 'I had plenty of time for thinking in the basement.' She pointed to Ruth's children, the Maibaum children, the Ehrlich boys, the Silbermann girls. 'They know all about it, so why not me? Do you think I can't stand the truth?'

Grandfather straightened out his crumpled handkerchief and put it to his eyes. Alice tore it out of his hands, rolled it into a ball and threw it on to the stinking heap. There it lay.

Grandfather put his face in his hands.

'They did it for love,' said Ruth quietly.

'They should never have lied to me,' sobbed Alice.

'If only one knew what was lies and what was the truth,' said Mr Blum. 'Who knows if what we now think is true really *is* the truth?'

'They knew they were lying!' cried Alice.

'I do know people,' said old Mr Cohn in the corner, 'whose children couldn't cope with the truth.'

Alice was still standing in front of her grandfather. He had now sunk down so far that his forehead was on his knees.

'I'm hungry,' she said.

Grandfather did not move.

'I'm hungry,' she shouted. 'Get up! You're sitting on the holdall!'

She shook him, and he tipped over sideways. Shocked, she tried to keep him upright, but his weight pushed her aside. Then he fell off the holdall on to the floor.

Paul came and bent over the crumpled body with Ruth. The blonde woman with the baby came closer, the curly-haired toddler clinging to her dress and whining. Mr Blum stepped across the luggage and moved Alice away. Almost the whole truck was now in motion, all crowding round Grandfather, even the Herschels.

Her heart thudding, Alice stood to one side, in the midst of overturned luggage. Only the pregnant woman and her husband had stayed in their corner and the singer had not moved from her case either. She turned her piercing eyes on Alice and put her hand on her breast, her face expressing sorrow. Then she smiled at Alice. It helped.

'Is there a nurse among us?' asked Mr Blum. 'A medical orderly?'

There was no answer. On someone else's rucksack Alice saw a large, folded slice of bread. Instinctively she grabbed it and stuffed the dripping-spread slice into her mouth. At the same time she felt a strong desire to strike out, or tear open the door and throw out all the cases, rucksacks and tied-up boxes that lay around her. Her heart was racing.

She was still chewing when the circle of helpers and onlookers opened up again and everyone returned silently to their places. Only Ruth and Mr Blum stayed beside Grandfather, who was now lying stretched out on the floor, directly in front of the sliding-door. Someone had pushed Alice's coat under his head. His own coat covered both face and body. Alice saw him lying there, but she did not move, was unaware of the murmuring voices and sympathetic looks.

Ruth came over to her and held her close. 'He is dead, Alice,' she said calmly. 'It was all too much for him. I was worried about him before, when he slept for such a long time.' And when Alice continued to stand there, stiff and silent, and did not respond to her hug, she said, 'You belong to us, now, the Mandels.'

She signalled to Rebekka, but when Rebekka tried to take Alice's hand, Alice snatched it back, went over to

Grandfather and bent over the dead body. She lifted the corner of the coat that lay over his face.

'He is not blaming you,' whispered Rebekka, trying to draw her away.

'Leave her,' Alice heard Ruth say.

Alice crouched beside Grandfather but did not cover his face again. There was silence in the truck, only the baby was crying and the youngest Maibaum whining. Looking up for a moment, she met furtively curious eyes. She felt under the coat and touched Grandfather's familiar hand. It was lifeless, but still warm. Alice took it in her own and held it against her. As if from a distance, she heard an excited exchange between Bull-neck and Mr Blum. It seemed to be about the space that Grandfather was now taking up, lying along the wall with the sliding-door in it, while the holdall and ruck-sack were on top of other pieces of luggage between Alice and the pregnant Mrs Wormser. Bull-neck and his girlfriend were now sitting close to the Wormsers.

But none of that concerned her. She was unable to think. She could only feel Grandfather's hand slowly growing cool.

Mrs Cohn, the old woman with the cross-stitched table-cloth, came clambering painfully up and stroked her hair. 'Just remember that it's over for him now. Who knows what is waiting for us, child. He doesn't have to go through it . . .'

Alice looked up at her and nodded. She thought of Grand-mother, who would know nothing of Grandfather's death – if she was still alive. If so, she would never be allowed to return home, nor would Mrs Lohmann.

Alice remembered now. The entrance door to the base-ment flat from the staircase had been walled up. A curtained doorway had led directly from Mrs Lohmann's storeroom into the kitchen and had an old carpet hanging over it; furni-ture, cases and rolls of cloth had been placed in front of it. When they had moved down to the cellar two years ago, she had been told it was because of the war. They would be safer in the cellar from the bombs. And as the war was certainly not going to last very long, they would soon be able to move up again. Meanwhile, Mrs Lohmann would live up above and keep those two floors in order.

What if a bomb should hit Mrs Lohmann? Alice had objected. Daddy's answer was that in an emergency, Mrs Lohmann would run down to the cellar. And Grandmother had added that Mrs Lohmann was a very brave woman.

It now seemed to Alice that this was the only little bit of truth in the whole story that had been dished up to her. Mrs Lohmann had taken over their house and had perhaps spread a rumour that the Dubskys had made their escape by night. Perhaps they had gone to another country – at all events, they had vanished without trace. In reality they, the Dubskys, were in the cellar of the house where she lived, protected by the big garden, Grandfather's walls in front of the windows, and Mrs Lohmann, who was not Jewish. Every night Grandfather had carefully lowered the black blinds in front of the windows. 'Against enemy bombers,' he had said, and of course that was true, but above all it was so that no one should become aware that Jews were still living in the basement of the former 'Jews' house'. Not one gleam of light had ever shown outside.

Everything was now so clear to Alice: the fear in the eyes of her parents and grandparents when, besides Mrs Lohmann's voice, men's loud voices could also be heard from the basement. Alice had run to the door to have a look, but Daddy had held her back, his finger to his lips. That meant *be as quiet as a mouse*. For a quarter of an hour they had sat on their beds without moving.

Long after the men's voices had moved away, Grandmother had gone to the kitchen to make coffee and the other three had told Alice that policemen had come looking for an escaped criminal. If they had seen Daddy or Grandfather, they might have thought they were the criminals and shot them.

Grandmother, knowing nothing about this explanation, had told her in the kitchen that they had been customs men, looking for hidden coffee. Alice remembered that even then she had suspected that neither story was true, but Mummy, Daddy and Grandfather had then admitted that Grandmother had been quite right, the criminal had been caught, they had been wrong. Then Alice had believed them again, and when Mrs Lohmann, still trembling, had come down they had embraced her and thanked her. That fitted the customs story.

The story about the dentist was probably true. Mummy's cheek had really been swollen and her pain was certainly not put on – but the dental clinic was a lie. Her parents had been caught by someone in the street and the police had discovered that they were Dubskys: Jews. Probably they had been transported, in a train very like this one, to a camp. They were sure to have been treated just as roughly and unkindly as Grandmother and Grandfather, or even worse.

And then a dreadful thought shot through her: had the police tried to find out from them where they had been hiding? Had they even been beaten to get it out of them? She did not dare to think about it. But if her parents had betrayed the basement hiding-place, she and her grandparents would probably have been picked up that night.

No one had come. No one had betrayed anything – at least not then. Alice started. Grandfather's hand was now quite cold. She held his head and shook it. 'Grandfather,' she cried, 'please forgive me! I won't do it again!'

Someone tried to pull her away, but she would not let go of Grandfather's head. She tried to pull him upright, but he was much too heavy and she only tore his shirt. She cried and cried, and could not stop until Ruth slapped her face. Then she let Grandfather's shirt slip from her clenched hands and fell silent. Her chin sank on to her chest.

The train clattered over railway points.

'Dresden!' Paul called out.

But the train did not stop. It travelled slowly through the station and got up speed again.

14

'Come on, child, drink,' Alice heard Ruth say. A hand touched her shoulder, straightened her up and held a mug to her lips.

She drank. It was ordinary water, luke-warm and stale.

'I'm thirsty too,' whined David.

'Thirsty . . . thirsty . . .' came other children's voices in the truck, like an echo.

'We must be very careful with the water,' Ruth told David. 'Just now Alice needs it more than you do, and our bottle is only half full.'

Ruth and Rebekka pushed the holdall between Alice and the dead man. 'Go to sleep, Alice,' whispered Rebekka.

But Alice could not sleep. She went on thinking about Mrs Lohmann, poor Mrs Lohmann. Now she too would be sent to a camp. How many camps could there be? Would there be any hope of meeting her there?

The house they had lived in had two floors with six rooms each, much too big for one person on her own. Grandmother and Grandfather had lived on the ground floor, because it was not so easy for them to go upstairs, and she had lived with her parents on the first floor, where they had a wonderful view of the town. Alice still remembered her room in detail, with its soft, flowered curtains which moved in the breeze when the window was open. Over her bed hung a toy clock, and when you pulled the cord it played sweetly 'Go to sleep, my baby' – like little drops of music.

Apart from her room, there was a living-room, a dining-room, a music room, a bedroom and Daddy's study. Up under the roof were two guest-rooms, and when her friends came to visit her, they could play all over the house, including the basement. In those days there was a gardener living in the basement. Mr Weinrich had been everything: gardener, caretaker and Grandmother's chauffeur.

Again Alice felt a hand on her shoulder, a man's hand. She started up as if electrified. Grandfather? Had it all been a dream?

It was Bull-neck, leaning over her. He was wearing a shirt now. He touched her face.

'Your grandad had a roll of toilet paper in his hand,' he whispered. 'We forgot to put in any paper. Can you help us out?'

Alice nodded, pulled the roll out of Grandfather's coat pocket and handed it to him. He did not thank her.

'We're going through Lausitz now,' Rebekka whispered.

Alice did not care where the train was going. In her thoughts she was moving from room to room on the upper floor of the white house, looking through an open window on to the garden, which was full of birdsong. Down there among the trees, the swing was moving on its ropes with soft sighing noises.

Suddenly the pregnant woman screamed piercingly. Ruth got up and went over to her, followed by Mrs Herz. They had to climb over Max and Moustache.

There was a disturbance among the Herschels too. Alice

straightened up and saw the three sisters trying to restrain their fat brother. He was complaining of thirst, but just as Samuel was about to open his water-bottle, Ernstl made a clumsy grab for it. Samuel was so surprised that Ernstl actually succeeded, but then Mr Ehrlich, the one with the beard and hat, jumped up, and he and his son tried to take back the bottle. There was a furious struggle. Then Alice saw the hat fly across the truck and a second later she heard the bottle break. Water sprayed out on all sides.

'And now?' roared Mr Ehrlich. 'That was our last water.'

He gave the fat Herschel a ringing box on the ear and the three Herschel sisters began to cry. 'Ernstl is just a child,' they moaned. 'What he sees, he wants!'

Meanwhile, Ernstl had thrown himself flat on the floor, kicking old Cohn in the face as he went. Alice craned her neck to see what he would do. He seemed to be trying to lick up the little puddle of water, while his three sisters tugged at him, trying to coax him up, but Samuel's father kicked him hard in the back and roared, 'Damned idiot!'

Mr Blum tried to make peace. He offered Mr Ehrlich and his sons half a mugful from his own bottle and the hat was handed across the truck, all the way back to its owner.

But almost immediately there came another wild shriek. As he got up, Ernstl had put his hand on the floor and cut himself on the glass fragments. Now he was bleeding, and crying like a small child. The sisters rummaged in their bags for a towel, wound it round the injured hand and tried to comfort their brother.

'He's a danger to the public,' said the trench-coat woman. 'That sort should be in a special truck!'

By now the Herschel sisters had squeezed their brother firmly between them. He was leaning against one sister and dozing off. The one who seemed to Alice to be the eldest got up and apologized. Ernstl was normally quite peaceful and she could not understand what had suddenly got into him. They would do all they could not to let anything like that happen again. And, turning to Mr Ehrlich, she added how sorry they were not to be able to replace his water. Ernstl had already drunk all the water from the four bottles they had brought with them. All they could offer him would be an empty bottle.

Alice saw Mr Ehrlich waving her angrily away. She wanted to think of home again, but she could not escape to the white house any more. The pregnant woman was now groaning so loudly that Alice could no longer concentrate. Mr Blum and Ruth bent over her, but Alice could not hear what they were saying. The red-cheeked woman handed her a mug of tea and her husband knelt in front of her, rubbing her feet.

Alice was surprised. Why was he rubbing her feet?

'She should lie down now,' said Mr Blum, so loudly that everyone could hear him. 'It might come quite suddenly.'

This time it was the Silbermanns who had to move, but they did not grumble. Mr Silbermann leaned against the wall beside the peeing crack; the mother and daughters sat between the Mandels and Bull-neck, who had to move again with his girlfriend – this time to the middle of the truck. Alice could hear him cursing under his breath.

Beside her David was crying. 'I keep thinking about Struppi,' he sobbed.

'Do be quiet,' Alice begged. 'Couldn't you all be quiet for a bit . . .'

Rebekka shrugged her shoulders sadly.

Alice turned round and leaned over the holdall. Grandfather's face looked whiter now, more dead. The wrinkles were very deep, the tear ducts like hillocks. The folds that ran from his nostrils to the corners of his mouth were like dried-out riverbeds, his slightly open mouth like a gulf. It was no longer a face but a dead landscape. Alice remembered that she had once asked him if he had killed people in the war, but he had evaded her question, had suddenly had something important to do.

She had not asked again. The answer would in any case have been no: her dear, good grandfather – how could anyone possibly imagine him killing other people?

She stood up and looked at him from above, at a greater distance, and from there the strange landscape of the dead face turned back into the familiar features of her beloved grandfather. She crouched beside him and stroked the cold cheeks. He was still there. She was not yet completely alone.

'Alice!' someone called. She looked up. Paul was beckoning her and she climbed over the luggage towards him.

'I wanted to show you the evening sky,' he said, lifting her up.

Outside, a lake landscape painted in flaming reds flowed past, the black outlines of weeping willows on the bank. The disc of the sun was reflected in the water. Anglers stood on a wooden quay, scarcely noticing the train rattling by. The air was cold and smelled wonderful.

For a moment Paul pressed his cheek tenderly to her temple. 'You will get over it, Alice,' he said quietly. 'You will see how much a human being can bear.'

Then he put her down again.

15

•••

As if under a spell, Alice returned to her place. She would have liked to keep her eye to the knothole as long as it was light outside, but Grandfather was lying in front of it and he must be left in peace. She no longer wanted to look into his face. With the dead man behind her, she leaned against the holdall again and closed her eyes. She wanted to retain the picture of the still lake at evening.

But she was not given much time. Ruth had returned from the corner where the pregnant woman lay to see to her own children. There was some pushing and shoving, David was crying, and Ruben complained that his foot had gone to sleep. Both of them wanted a drink. 'Just *something*, Ruth!'

A beam of red light shone through the grating, falling on Ruth as she leaned over David, then on the Herschels and Mr Blum, then moving across the truck again. Alice craned forward to see Mrs Wormser, the pregnant woman. Mrs Herz and Mrs Silbermann were both attending to her, wiping the sweat from her face and moistening her lips. Everyone was thirsty. The three youngest Maibaums were wailing; even the curly-haired toddler was sobbing; Ernstl was shouting for water at regular intervals. And she herself could not help thinking of the everlastingly dripping tap in the basement kitchen. If only she could be there now, at home! Grandmother would have made tea for her right away.

She felt the tears running down her cheeks.

'How about playing cards as long as it's light?' asked Ruth, looking at Alice.

'Play cards!' cried the singer. 'The child lost her grandfather two hours ago and you ask her if she wants to play cards!'

'In this truck an hour is a year,' said Ruth very quietly.

Alice did not understand that, but it must have enraged the singer, because she hissed angrily, 'Oh, hold your tongue!'

But neither David nor Ruben wanted to play cards. Ruth put the pack away again in silence.

'Why don't you read to us?' begged David. 'You have brought the book.' Ruth nodded.

David sat up and cried, 'My mother is going to read a fairy-tale!'

It was not long before ten children were crowded round Ruth. The youngest was the toddler, the eldest Alice.

'*Once upon a time there was a little girl whose father and mother had died,*' began Ruth, '*and she was so poor that she had no room to live in and no bed to sleep on, and in the end, no more than the clothes on her back . . .*'

Oh, yes, the Star Thaler child. The living-room in Grandmother's and Grandfather's floor of the house appeared before her eyes. There had been so many children there, school friends and neighbours' children. In the old days Mummy had rehearsed a little play with them: *The Tale of the Star Thalers*. Then it was Grandfather's birthday, and at last they could perform it. Alice had been the Star Thaler child and most of the other children had dressed up as stars. At the end of the play they all danced round Alice, tossing silver thalers into her white skirt – only not real coins, but delicious chocolate money wrapped in shiny foil. Daddy accompanied the dancers on the piano. Grandfather had been very moved and had clapped for a long time.

But Alice could not think of that wonderful day without being reminded of the dreadful November night as well. It was a week after Grandfather's birthday. Alice had been awakened by her room being brilliantly lit up. Alice called to her parents, who were playing music together, and pointed excitedly at the window. Grandfather and Grandmother had come upstairs too and they all gazed, bewildered, at the town. The synagogue was burning, the big, beautiful synagogue which they always passed on their way to Grandfather's coffee business. The whole town, the whole sky was brilliantly lit by the blaze – even the walls of her room were illuminated. Grandfather had clenched his hands in his trouser pockets, as she could see. Grandmother cried, and Daddy and Mummy held each others' hands.

Alice had been to the synagogue two or three times with her grandparents. Mummy and Daddy did not go. She had sat upstairs with her grandmother, while Grandfather stayed downstairs with the men. She could still remember the great, stately room. The fact that all four grown-ups were now so distressed could mean only that someone had set fire to the synagogue. But when she asked, her father told her, 'No, Mousie, no one does anything as mean as that. It must have been lightning.'

Although Alice was then only eight years old, she knew that lightning came with a storm – and there had been no storm. And Mummy, who could sometimes read people's thoughts, added hastily, 'It could even have been a spark from the railway – it's windy today.'

After that night Daddy would not let her go to school. She was given lessons at home for over a year by a Mrs Rosenheimer. To begin with her school friends used to visit her, but gradually they faded away, in the end even Trudi. 'I'm not allowed to come any more,' she said sadly, 'because you are Jews.'

Alice had begged again and again to be allowed to go back to school, but Daddy, who usually gave her everything she asked for, had been determined. 'Believe me,' he had told her very seriously, 'for now it will be best for you to stay at home. Later on you will understand . . .'

'*And after she had walked on a little way,*' Ruth continued, '*there came another child, who had no bodice and was freezing, so she gave away her own . . .*'

Since that November night, it seemed to Alice, everything had been different, somehow grim and gloomy. The day before the fire, Grandmother had given her a beautiful white skating costume, fringed with fur. By now it was too small for her, although she had been unable to wear it even once, because she was not allowed to go to the skating rink any more. And then Grandfather and Daddy sold the whole coffee wholesale business to Mrs Lohmann, and they too stayed at home. Alice had been very upset. She loved going to the coffee warehouse, where it was such fun playing hide-and-seek among the sacks, parcels and shelves.

'Grandfather can't bear the dust in the storerooms any more,' Mummy had explained. How extraordinary – all of a sudden!

'*At last she came to a forest,*' Ruth read, '*and it was already dark, when yet another child came, asking for a shift – and the kind little girl thought: "It is a dark night, no one will see you, you can quite well give away your shift," and she gave that away too . . .*'

One day Daddy no longer had a car. Grandmother and Mummy did not go to the shops where they had once been customers – for instance, to the greengrocer's, where Alice had always been given a tangerine. Mrs Lohmann now did the shopping for them – and there were fewer and fewer visitors. So many friends and old acquaintances of Daddy and Mummy and her grandparents were leaving the country. At last even Mrs Rosenheimer left. Grandfather explained to Alice that she had gone to live with relations in America. From then on Mummy and Daddy had taught her, and sometimes Grandfather too.

'*And as she stood there, no longer having anything at all, the stars began to fall from the sky, as hard, shiny thalers; and although she had given away her shift, she was suddenly wearing a new shift, made of the finest linen . . .*'

They had always given a clear explanation of everything, all of them, including the mysterious move to the basement. And she had believed them and trusted them blindly and had had no idea what had been going on outside the white house.

It had become very lonely in the basement.

The story of the star thalers was over. The sun had set and the truck was growing darker. Outside, a beautiful early autumn day had come to an end. All Alice had seen of it was the dawn and a few sections framed by the knothole and the gratings. 'If everything was as it was a long time ago,' she thought, 'today would have been a holiday for me, and I would have gone to the swimming-pool with Trudi, or spent the day with Uncle Ludwig and Aunt Irene. Or I might simply have sat on the swing, reading in the garden . . .'

Now Ruth was reading another fairy-tale aloud. It was called *The Water of Life*, and Alice did not know it. She noticed that everyone was listening with interest, including the pregnant woman, Mr Blum and even Bull-neck. Grandfather would surely have been listening too.

The story was about a king who was close to death, and

his three sons, crying for him in the garden of the palace. An old man asked the reason for their grief and gave them a little hope: '*I know a remedy, the water of life; if he drinks that he will be well again. But it is hard to find . . .*'

The pregnant woman, Mrs Wormser, suppressed a groan, but the baby was beginning to cry. Ruth interrupted the story and waited until the blonde woman had put the child to her breast.

'Go on,' someone called.

Ruth went on reading. '*Now the eldest son rode out into the world to find the water, but because he was thinking of his own interests, he got stuck in a ravine that was so narrow that he could no longer even turn his horse.*' The same thing happened to the second son.

Mrs Wormser could not help groaning again, but she pressed a towel to her mouth so that the others could go on listening. They heard that the youngest son was the only one who rode out with a pure heart, simply to help his sick father; he was worthy to find the way to the water of life.

'*It springs from a fountain in the courtyard of an enchanted castle, but you will not get in unless I give you an iron rod and two loaves of bread. Beat three times with the rod on the iron door of the castle and it will spring open. Inside are two lions with gaping jaws, but if you throw each of them a loaf they will keep still. Then hurry and collect the water of life before the clock strikes twelve, otherwise the gate will close and you will be a prisoner.*'

After much trouble the youngest son succeeded in finding the water. Scarcely had the old king drunk it than he felt his sickness fall away and he became strong and tall as in his youth . . .

'And a story like that isn't going to make you thirsty?' said Max, who was now on his feet again, leaning against the wall by the other grating.

The baby began to cry, and the blonde woman cried too;

she had no milk left. It was almost impossible to see anything in the truck. Lights from a station flickered through the gratings, travelled across the walls and vanished. Someone cursed – evidently because he had trodden in the heap in the darkness.

16

•••

The train gave a jolt and the buffers slammed into each other. Once again light fell through the gratings, brushed along the wall and went out. The train slowed down, with much creaking, rattling and screeching, and stopped.

'Lia, Lia!' came the cry from the next truck.

Max and Moustache jumped up.

'We are in a goods station,' Paul called out.

'Water!' cried the blonde woman.

The people in the neighbouring trucks also began to shout. 'There's a dead body here!' shouted Mr Blum.

Paul joined in. 'There's a dead body here! And a woman in labour!' Their voices tumbled over each other.

'Which side is the platform?' asked Moustache quickly.

'It's not here,' said Max, his face to the bars.

'Not here either,' Paul reported from the other grating. 'We seem to be in a siding.'

Alice wondered what was going on.

On the platform someone blew a whistle, men's voices shouted orders, a dog barked. Max and Moustache bumped their heads together at their grating. One growled 'Watch out!' and the other cursed under his breath. Then they pushed their way through to Paul. Bull-neck also climbed over Ruth and the children to reach Paul. The corner where they stood was getting crowded. The baby cried.

'Careful!' cried Paul, 'Mind the children!'

Then they all shouted: 'Open up! Open up! Water! Doctors!'

Everyone who was close to a wall drummed on it with fists, shoes, anything that made a noise. In the light that came through the gratings, Alice could now see the four young men standing near the sliding-door, craning their necks. She shook with fright. What would happen to Grandfather's body if the door opened?

After a time there was a rattle – but on the other side of the truck. The peeing crack opened, the sliding-door rolled thunderously to one side and into the heap of excrement that had piled up against the wall.

'Filthy muck!' Alice heard a man's voice growl.

The Herschels, who had not realized that the door was going to open on their side this time, began to shriek. Ernstl had obviously not been quick enough to grasp that there was now no wall behind him. Alice saw him fall out as his sisters screamed.

Ruth, Rebekka, the trench-coat pair, the Maibaums – all jumped up and started shouting at once. In the midst of this chaos, the four young men rushed to the door, pushed aside the people leaning out and jumped off the truck. Alice saw them running across the rails.

She was rooted to the floor. Outside there were shots, then searchlights blazed, and now everyone was on their feet, crowding to the door. Alice could no longer see what was happening. She was aware only of the shots, cries and men's voices bellowing. Behind her, Bull-neck's red-cheeked girlfriend was wailing, 'No, Bruno – they'll do you in!'

'Good for you, Max!' Alice heard Mrs Herz murmur. 'That was your chance.' But she saw the woman's fingers twisting, her palms pressed together.

Two uniformed men threw Ernstl back into the truck. His sisters bent over him with loud, lamenting cries, touching and stroking him. 'Thank God!' cried one of them. He seemed to have survived his fall unharmed.

But why had the truck fallen silent? Alice craned her neck. She could not see what they were all looking at.

'Wonder if the others made it,' said someone softly.

'Who is it?' asked Mrs Herz, choking.

'Oh, no!' said another woman's horrified voice.

Two uniformed men thrust in a lifeless body and disappeared. Ruth, who had been standing near the door, turned to Alice and put her arms round her.

'Paul,' she murmured. 'They have shot Paul.'

Mr Blum and Mr Ehrlich carried the dead man over to Alice's grandfather, pushed away the holdall and laid Paul down beside him. When a beam of light touched the dead man, Alice could see that his chest and temples were covered with blood. His eyes were wide open.

'Sit somewhere else, child,' Mr Blum told Alice, but she went on standing beside Paul, looking into his face. Ruth tried to pull her away.

'Leave me alone,' she said roughly.

'Bruno!' wailed Bull-neck's girlfriend. 'What shall I do now?'

Mrs Herz went over to her, stooped down and said, 'Be glad for him. Think what he's been spared, him and my Max and the other one.'

'But what will become of me?' the red-cheeked girl whispered.

Mrs Herz turned away. 'Who knows what good it did,' she said, pointing to Paul. 'I had always wanted a dream son like him – and my Max was quite different.'

'Is Max your son then?' asked Alice.

Mrs Herz nodded. 'We never got on very well,' she said. 'Till now. I would never have thought he had so much courage. It was fear that did it. My Max – may all good spirits protect him.' With that she pushed her way between the others.

Alice felt terribly alone. Everyone else had crowded back to the open door. Light fell on the toilet corner. The sticky mush gleamed, now licking its way with greedy tongues towards the luggage.

A quarter of an hour ago Paul had still been alive, and now nobody cared about him any more. Alice no longer understood her world. 'Paul's dead!' she shouted. 'Do you hear?'

'Yes,' cried Samuel, 'but now we need water!'

Mr Blum leaned out and signalled to someone. 'There's a woman giving birth in here!' he shouted.

'So?' Alice heard a man's voice say. And then several men laughed. Alice had scarcely time to be indignant, because things were happening everywhere, all the time. Once again the shouts for water came, this time from the next truck. Everyone joined in and shouted until they could shout no longer.

'We need a doctor or a nurse!' cried Mr Blum.

'Stay in there or you're for it!' came the voice from outside. And a moment later the same voice said, 'It stinks to high heaven here.'

Once again they heard shots, this time further away, somewhere in the railway precincts. 'Bruno, Bruno,' moaned Bull-neck's girlfriend.

Suddenly a man in uniform appeared at the door opening and snarled, 'Two out to fetch water!'

Samuel jumped out of the truck but was pushed back in again. It had to be two of the older men. So Mr Blum and Mr Maibaum went.

At great speed, vessels were hauled out of the luggage, soap was unpacked. Suddenly there was a towel hanging on a nail. Everything had to be done in the feeble light that came in through the door. 'Yes, now you'll have a wash, sweetheart,' Alice heard the blonde say tenderly.

'If they bring enough we'll even be able to clean the corner,' said someone.

'Still believe in miracles?' asked another voice.

The pregnant woman was screaming with pain again, and her husband, little Mr Wormser, risked climbing out of the truck. Alice heard his weak voice calling, 'Where is the guard? I must talk to the guard. It's urgent.'

'What the devil,' somebody roared, 'what the devil is this gnome doing out here?'

'But my –' Mr Wormser began, then those who were standing near the opening jumped back. Alice could clearly see the little man being picked up under the arms by two uniformed men and thrown headfirst into the truck to the sound of laughter. He knocked over a couple of children who had pushed forward inquisitively and then fell full-length over a case. Alice heard glass breaking.

'My glasses!' Mr Wormser protested.

His sleeves had been torn off and his shirt was hanging out of his trousers. He wept despairingly. Mr Silbermann tried to calm him down and led him to his wife in the corner. Weeping, she flung her arms round his neck.

'Sarah,' he sobbed.

Alice could not look, or she too would have begun to cry. She could feel the lump in her throat. She pushed her way to the door opening and peered outside. What a line of trucks! From far back she heard the shout: 'A doctor! A doctor!'

When she looked the other way she saw a small, delicate woman, no longer young, climbing out of the next truck. She hurried along the train to the opening where Alice was standing, lifted her head and pleaded, 'Have you seen my daughter? We were together on the platform, but she wanted to go to the toilet, and before she got back I had to get in. Her name is Lia, nine years old. Short brown hair and a bright blue dress –'

Alice shook her head. 'She's not in here.' Tears sprang to her eyes.

The woman went on asking her question from truck to truck.

At the fifth truck she was stopped and two guards pushed her roughly inside. Her cries could be heard throughout the station.

'But that's not where she should be,' said Alice.

'Does it matter?' asked Rebekka, who was standing behind her.

Alice noticed a little note lying on the gravel under the grating. Probably no one would find it, or the rain would finally wash away the writing. None of the railway men or guards would take the trouble to pick it up. No one would find out what had happened in these cattle trucks, until one day, perhaps after many years, the Jews came home from the camps in the east.

At that moment Mr Blum and Mr Maibaum reappeared between the buildings, left the crowd of other water-carriers, now struggling off in all directions, and returned to their truck. Each was carrying a large bucket, from which water slopped.

'One for drinking, one for washing,' said Mr Blum, lifting his bucket into the truck. 'And keep to your turn!'

'But that's not nearly enough,' cried the blonde woman. 'There are almost fifty of us in here.'

'Hurry up,' said Mr Maibaum. 'Perhaps we'll be allowed . . .'

First came the drinking water. How to fill the vessels – there was no funnel. To be filled they had to be held under the water, and the water was getting dirtier all the time. And when the bucket was empty, not nearly everyone in the truck had filled their bottles. The water from the second bucket also had to be used for drinking – drinking was naturally more important than washing. But the blonde woman was in despair. 'The baby's so sore,' she complained.

And what was to happen to the pregnant woman? What water could they use for her?

'Just one more bucketful,' Mr Blum begged a uniformed man passing by.

The man looked up, spat and then nodded. 'Get on then, but quick. And take both buckets, man. If you're doing it, do it properly!'

Mr Blum and Mr Maibaum ran off with their buckets, accompanied by this one human human being, with a gun on his back. But the engine was already whistling. One truck after another was slammed shut and bolted. At the last moment the two water-carriers came back, pushed the buckets into the truck and climbed in after them. Mr Maibaum almost knocked Alice over.

But where could they put the water in such a hurry? The buckets had to be left at this station – they were already standing out on the platform in irregular rows, the full length of the train. The only gap was in front of their truck.

The uniformed man stole a glance to either side. Then he growled, 'For God's sake, they can stay in there then! We're not going to lose the war for two lousy buckets.'

He slammed the door shut and bolted it from the outside.

'God bless you!' called Mr Blum.

'God? Ha, ha!' came the reply from outside.

Everyone breathed a sigh of relief, although it was now almost dark in the truck. 'We were in luck,' someone said.

'But Paul,' said Alice loudly, 'Paul is dead. And who knows – perhaps the others too . . .'

'Psst!' went somebody.

Rebekka, still standing behind Alice, burst into a storm of weeping.

'Stop, stop!' she sobbed.

Alice was reaching for her hand when the train jolted away again. She heard splashing and at the same time felt cold water on her right ankle. She realized that the jolt had sent water splashing out of the bucket beside her, of which she could see a faint outline. But then even the faint light from the last station lamp passed by the grating and she could no longer see the bucket at all.

17

Now, before most people had had time to return from the door to their places, it was completely dark in the truck.

'The buckets! Careful! The buckets!' Alice heard Mr Blum shouting. His voice was quite close to her. Alice bent and, as she felt for the bucket, her hands plunged straight into the water. But where was the other one? She grasped someone's leg – then she had it, the second bucket. She pulled it close against the other, shielding the first with her body and hugging the second in her arms.

She was going to call out to Mr Blum when someone's foot met her head. It was horribly painful and was immediately followed by another kick. She gave a scream, drew back her sore head and dipped it in the bucket to escape the blows. They must think she was just a piece of luggage in the way!

Shouts flew to and fro: 'Where are you, Mum?' – 'Over here, Ilse' – 'I can't get out of here' – 'Stay where you are and wait for some light' – 'Mama, come here!' and a desperate 'Benni!'

The water was cool on her chin and nose, deliciously cool.

Her face was in the water that was slopping to and fro in the bucket, and she could not resist the temptation to dip her whole head in it.

'Where are the buckets?' she heard Mr Blum calling excitedly.

Alice meant to keep her face in the water for just one more second. Just one single second.

'They must be somewhere!' cried Mr Blum.

One more second. And then temptation overcame her so powerfully that she opened her mouth and drank – hastily, one swallow after another. Three deep gulps. On the third she choked and had to cough.

'Alice –' she heard Ruth's voice, 'Where are you, child?'

'The buckets, everyone. We must pass the water round!' Mr Blum shouted furiously.

Alice had caught her breath again. 'They're here, Mr Blum,' she called. 'I've got them. I'm lying across them.'

'Stay there,' she heard him reply. 'I'm coming.'

Children wailed. Alice could feel little groping hands and heard a pitiful 'Mummy!'

'Benni, Benni,' came the blonde woman's anxious response.

Two more kicks, then Alice felt the groping hands again. A woman's voice whispered above her, 'Is that you, Alice? Just let me have a mug full . . .'

Alice did not recognize the voice. 'No,' she said.

Then she felt a firm grip on her head, on her hair, trying to pull her away.

'No!' hissed Alice furiously.

A second voice joined in, a voice she knew. It was the trench-coat man. 'Just you wait, and I'll . . .' he whispered.

A torch went on, its beam wavering across the roof. Alice lifted her head. 'Mr Blum, Mr Blum!' she called.

And there he was. There he was, helping Alice on to her

feet. He praised her and she lowered her eyes quickly. Could he not see her wet face and hair? Didn't he guess that she had drunk some of the water – water which was not hers?

Mr Silbermann had come with Mr Blum, his tie under his ear. He took one of the two buckets and carried it across to the blonde woman, who had now found her Benni again in the wandering light of the torch. Mr Blum lit the way for Mr Silbermann. 'But only a quarter of it, a quarter at most!' he called. 'The rest must go to Mrs Wormser.' And then he shouted loudly across the truck, 'Who has another torch? We need light for the birth.'

Alice answered, and two more voices joined in hesitantly.

But there were more than four torches in the truck; one would light up here and there and then go out again. Alice felt her way to her little rucksack, groped in it for Grandfather's torch and handed it to Rebekka, who passed it on. So it found its way to the corner where Mrs Wormser lay groaning.

Soon that corner began to light up, shadows dancing on the roof. Backs and heads, black against the brightness, prevented Alice from seeing the young woman. One head, one back belonged to Ruth.

'Come on, Alice. Sit down,' said Rebekka beside her.

'We shall have to squash up now,' said Ruben. 'There's not much room left. The shit is only a step away.'

'We are three people less than when we left,' said Rebekka, 'but the dead take up so much room.'

'Now we have a whole bottle of water again,' murmured David, half asleep.

'Minus three swallows,' Ruben added, 'which Ruth let us have. How much water did you get?'

Alice thought of her three swallows and felt herself blushing. 'Our bottle is broken,' she said uncertainly. 'And there is still some coffee in the Thermos –'

'Just what I thought,' said Ruben grimly. 'Now Ruth will give you some of our water again.'

'You can keep your water,' said Alice sharply, then she pushed the holdall between herself and the Mandels and leaned against it, so that the Mandels were behind her, the dead in front of her. She had so little room that she had to draw her legs right up against her body. Behind her she could hear Rebekka scolding Ruben in a low voice.

'But it's true,' she heard Ruben answer defiantly.

Alice felt very much alone. Lost in thought, she began to divide her hair in two. She held one half, divided that into three and began to plait.

Her friend Trudi had had plaits as well, thin rat-tails, but with big bows holding them together. Trudi, whom she had sat next to at school until that dreadful November day. Trudi's parents had a milk and cheese shop, which was why Trudi always had cheese in her sandwiches. The cheese tasted so good that Alice often exchanged sandwiches with Trudi. Sometimes, when Mummy picked her up from school, she would say: 'You're smelling of Trudi again. Wouldn't you rather sit next to some other girl?'

But she had never wanted to sit next to anyone else. Trudi had told her a lot about her family life: her five brothers and sisters, and the shop, and the customers, and her parents – her fat father, who laughed a lot, and her fat mother, who was always 'suckling'. This had meant nothing to Alice in those days, but for some reason she had been shy of asking.

A light flitted across Paul's face. He was still staring at the ceiling with wide-open eyes. In the evening sunlight he had leaned his head against her temple and she had felt his hands on her waist when he lifted her up. She could still hear the sound of his laughter.

Alice went on plaiting. The plait stuck out rather crookedly behind her ear and it was very stiff, but it was a plait.

Now all she needed was a ribbon to hold it together. She rummaged in the holdall and rucksack, but although Grandmother had thought of everything, she had not thought of plait ribbons.

Suddenly she was holding the coloured scarf that Grandmother had knitted for her last birthday. She could feel the cap with the bobble on it as well. So Grandmother had already been thinking of next winter when she was packing. Alice pulled a thick piece of wool out of the bobble, wound it round the end of the plait and knotted it. It was not at all easy, in the semi-darkness, with the wool always slipping out of her fingers.

The whole rucksack was still full of food – how long was it since she had eaten? She had been only thirsty all the time. No, once she had felt a savage hunger, just after Grandfather died.

She could still see Paul's eyes when a beam of torchlight passed across his face. She turned to the red-cheeked woman, who was leaning against the wall with her eyes closed. She had pushed her case between herself and the dead bodies. Alice touched her, and the woman jumped and looked up.

'Can you shut Paul's eyes?' asked Alice.

For a short time it was pitch dark again.

'Me?' asked the woman. 'His eyes?' Alice could hear from her voice how horrified she was. 'I have never touched a dead body. Up to now I had never even seen a dead person . . .'

A beam of light flickered over them and Alice saw the woman leaning over the case and then drawing back with a shudder.

Now Alice divided the other half of her hair into three and began to plait. The second plait was going to come further forward. She let go of the strands and began again.

Paul. Now there was no one calling out the names of the stations, and no one seemed to be bothering about Alice.

Were they all exhausted? She suddenly noticed how tired she was herself.

Only this morning she could never have imagined sitting calmly beside two dead bodies, combing her hair and thinking about food. She leaned over towards the red-cheeked woman and whispered; 'If you just look at them long enough, it doesn't feel so bad.'

But the woman turned her head away, unwilling to listen.

Alice leaned over Paul and felt his face in the darkness. His eyelids were cool, dry and flexible. One after the other, she slid the lids down over his eyes, but in the flickering light she saw that they had opened again.

She looked round. No one seemed to have noticed what she was doing. She plaited the second bunch of hair, this time further back, and then with both hands she tried to close both of Paul's eyelids at the same time. This time she succeeded and his eyes stayed shut.

It was as simple as that. The red-cheeked woman could not do it, although she was two or three times as old as Alice.

Alice unpacked a sandwich and began to eat, slowly and thoughtfully, enjoying it. Grandfather was dead. Now there was no one to make decisions for her. Paul was dead, but in the camp she would meet many other boys. The basement was in the past; real life was about to begin, even if it was to be life in a camp.

She leaned back and watched the play of light on the ceiling. But then Mr Blum hung two torches on strings against the wall in the Wormsers' corner, so that they shone downwards. Soon only that corner was lit; the rest of the space lay in semi-darkness. Mrs Wormser groaned. Ruth was with her again now and Mrs Herz was also busy in the corner.

Trudi had five brothers and sisters. There was always so much going on in their home and Alice had envied her, but when she asked Mummy if she could have a little brother or sister, Mummy's eyes had filled with tears. The times were so difficult. When they improved, she and Daddy would be glad to order a little brother or sister for her.

Ha, ha, ha! 'Order!' Now she knew. She had been six then, now she was almost twice as old. The times had not improved, they had worsened, and still she had no little brother or sister. She had no parents either. She would probably never have a little brother or sister.

Mrs Wormser screamed and Alice looked across the truck. She could not see much. The woman was lying on the floor and there was luggage all round her. Alice could see only Mr Wormser, standing blinking without his glasses. She thought of Mummy, in that corner. No, that she could not imagine!

She looked quickly across at Paul and pulled Grandfather's coat over his face. What did it matter if Grandfather's feet were no longer covered? 'None of you deserved Paul,' she said in a low voice. 'You've already forgotten him. I shall never forget him . . .'

18

•••

Alice had imagined dead people as something to be afraid of – horrible in some way. But these two dead people were familiar to her. In some unknown place at the end of their journey, they would be buried, probably side by side. Alice would tend their graves lovingly, with rows of beautifully painted stones as a border and two big flat stones at the head on which she could scratch their names. There were stones everywhere.

She thought of the three little graves in the garden at home. In one of them she had buried her white mouse, which she had found one day lying stiff and lifeless in its cage. In another lay Grandmother's canary, and the third belonged to Prussi, the dachshund. Alice had looked after the three faithfully until they moved to the basement. Mrs Lohmann had always assured her that she went on looking after them, but Alice doubted that now. Why should they not have lied to her about that as well?

She had been barely six years old when Prussi died. She had planted the graves with dandelions, which stayed bright for a long time. Grandmother had wrinkled her nose. Since when did you plant weeds on graves? But how could the dandelion do anything about being called a weed? It was prettier than many garden plants. Grandfather had agreed, suppressing a smile: Yes, yes, you could look at it like that.

HERE LIES THE BODY OF SIEGFRIED DUBSKY
HERE LIES THE BODY OF PAUL . . .

What was Paul's surname? She must ask Mr Blum. Perhaps Paul was also one of those Jews who did not want flowers on their graves. Grandfather had explained that to her once, but she had not understood. She had never really been able to understand what made Jews different from other people.

Perhaps she would have to work so hard in this camp that she would have no time to look after the two graves. Well, in any case she would have time to think about the dead.

Paul had travelled alone. Would anyone be thinking of him? Parents? Brothers or sisters? A girlfriend? Her head against his temple – that had been lovely. While she worked, she would always think of him, or at least most of the time. A dead person is not really dead until no one is thinking of him, Grandmother had told her. And she wanted to think about Grandfather too, but she would not have to make a special effort to do that . . .

To the right, water splashed and the baby made gurgling sounds. The blonde woman spoke softly to him.

Yes, soon a completely new life would begin, a life in which she was worth just as much as a grown-up. A life full of work. She would be learning new things from morning till night.

She rummaged in the rucksack for the bag of oatcakes and put one in her mouth. She was quite surprised at her own appetite.

'Got something for me?' asked a girl's voice from the darkness.

It must be one of the Maibaum daughters. They had not yet spoken to her, although they were sitting only a few steps from her, behind a stack of cases. She must be very hungry.

'You can have the rest,' said Alice, holding out the bag into the darkness. Someone took it from her, and then began an eager toing and froing among the Maibaums.

Grandmother had packed food for three, and now Alice had it all to herself. Much too much. She opened another bag which contained long, dark biscuits that tasted of coffee. 'Coffee bones,' Grandfather had called them. Alice had helped to bake them. Grandmother had used coffee grounds to make up the dough, always baking for the future.

'Have you got anything for us?' asked Ruben sleepily from behind the holdall. 'Ruth won't give us any more today.'

Alice did not want to be mean, although Ruben had annoyed her. She reached into the bag. 'Hold out your hands,' she said, putting a handful of coffee bones in them. The three Silbermann girls got the rest. Grandfather would have been much more careful with the hand-outs, thought Alice. He was always thinking of tomorrow, but tomorrow was still so far away.

'Is that you, Alice, handing things out?' called Mrs Grün. 'Have you got anything left? Our little ones are not usually so hungry . . .'

Alice had some rusks, two packets of them, old stuff, all crumbled now. Grandfather had always teased Grandmother about her rusk stores. 'Iron rations,' he had called them. Alice handed Mrs Grün one packet and Mr Grün thanked her warmly.

'Alice,' called Samuel, 'if you've got a few crumbs left . . . we would be eternally grateful.' He giggled. 'Right, Aaron?'

'Leave her alone,' Alice heard Aaron say roughly.

All the same, she handed over the rest of the rusks. She was so full that she could not imagine eating anything more on this journey. But the coffee bones had made her thirsty. She took the Thermos out of the holdall and drank some. The Thermos was still half full. The coffee smelled of Grandmother, of the basement flat, in fact of the whole of Grandfather's coffee business, and she did not want to give any of it away. She crouched low over the holdall to drink it and quickly screwed the top back on the Thermos.

Light fell through the grating across Alice and moved over the truck. Ruth came back to her place from the Wormsers. Her movements showed how tired and sad she was. 'She is in so much pain,' she told Rebekka. 'Now she's freezing.' She pulled a knitted cardigan out of her luggage.

'Where are we, Ruth?' asked Rebekka.

'How should I know?' said Ruth. 'It doesn't matter, anyway.' And after a time she said, 'Watch out, the muck is coming. You will have to move.'

She leaned close to Alice and said, 'Could you lend Sarah Wormser your grandfather's coat until tomorrow morning? It looks so soft and warm. If she was lying on it she might feel better.'

Alice nodded without thinking. She stood up, took the coat off the two dead men and handed it over. It was heavy. Ruth thanked her and took the coat and cardigan back to Sarah Wormser.

The dead lay in deep shadow, but Alice knew that they were now uncovered, as if they had already been given up. She rummaged hastily in the holdall and took out anything suitable for a covering: two of her own dresses, two of Grandmother's, trousers and a pullover of Grandfather's. She spread the clothes carefully over the dead men, taking special care to cover their heads.

It grew colder. She put on her coat and wound the scarf round her neck. Was it midnight yet? She waited in vain for a light from outside so that she could read the time on her watch.

When she tried to lean back against the holdall, she realized it was now half empty and flabby. Alice pushed it close to Paul's head, stuffed her rucksack, which was also half empty, inside it, and used both as a pillow. Now she had enough room to sleep. She was now lying side-by-side with Paul.

'It looks as if you are dead too,' whispered Rebekka, leaning on Ruth's rucksack. Ruben's and David's heads were in her lap. Alice imagined how uncomfortable that must be for her.

'Rebekka?' came a soft voice from further back.

'Who's that?' asked Rebekka.

It was Aaron. He scrambled over and crouched beside Rebekka. 'I believe,' Alice heard him saying very quietly, 'they're going to kill us there. I have the feeling that we are all going to die . . .'

Alice listened fearfully. What did he mean? When they had had the great flu epidemic, Grandmother had wailed, 'We shall all be done for!' But Grandfather had burst out laughing.

'Nonsense,' said Rebekka calmly, almost cheerfully. 'If they killed us, that would mean that they were killing all the other Jews too. There are millions of Jews in Europe, Ruth told us. You can't kill millions except in a war. They would have to kill us secretly, without being seen. I bet you can't tell me how they would do that.' She shook her head. 'Things like that don't happen.'

Alice breathed a sigh of relief.

'You are right,' said Aaron thoughtfully, 'it's impossible . . .'

Now Alice joined in the conversation. 'Rebekka,' she asked, 'what is so bad about us Jews that the others don't want us?'

'We are too clever for them,' said Rebekka. 'It makes them envious.'

'We have learned a lot,' added Aaron, 'because we have always been persecuted and had to fight for our lives. Do you know what pogroms are? Jews were killed in them, in hundreds, sometimes in thousands. Executed, beaten, burned. We Jews were always scapegoats. We were even accused of being responsible for the plague.'

'The plague?' asked Alice, astonished. 'But that was a long time ago . . .'

'There have been pogroms in almost every century,' whispered Aaron. 'In Spain, in Italy and here. That way we learned to adapt and find loopholes, but also to be able to do more than other people.'

Alice thought of the burning of the synagogue and it was as if scales had fallen from her eyes: Mummy, Daddy and her grandparents had been afraid.

'We are simply different,' said Rebekka. 'That's why we are always the scapegoats.'

'I wish I wasn't a Jew,' sighed Alice. 'Everything would be all right then. I would be able to go to school with the others and we would still be living on the upper floors. My parents wouldn't have needed to lie to me. If we were not Jews, we could all be at home – alive!'

'Would, could,' said Rebekka angrily. 'Well, you are Jewish and you always will be.'

'I don't think much has changed since the plague,' said Aaron. 'They even tell their little children that the Jews are the devil and that Hitler is something like a god. Always! And they tell everyone that they are sure of final victory and that the Third Reich will last a thousand years . . .'

'According to them, we are cowardly, malicious and only after money,' said Rebekka.

'I hope,' said Aaron, 'that in this war, which they started, they will die like flies. I hope their houses will be bombed and burned and that lots of their children won't be born – children they would have had if they had kept the peace. I hope many of them will lose their homes and families, and above all I hope other countries will feel loathing for them. I wouldn't be one of them for anything in the world.'

'I'm proud of being a Jew,' said Rebekka.

'Me too,' sighed Aaron, 'but sometimes I shake with fear. They call us pests that have to be wiped out, and sometimes I think that one day they'll really do it. Then I wish I were a bedouin or an Indian. But then, when I'm over my fear, like now, I can't imagine being anything but a Jew.'

'Sleep, boy,' growled Mr Ehrlich. 'You're disturbing the others.'

Aaron stopped talking and climbed back to his place.

Rebekka moved closer to Alice. 'I dream of a country,' she whispered, 'where only Jews live. How lovely that would be. A peaceful country . . .'

Alice thought of her friend Trudi, who was not Jewish. Trudi would not be there if she were in a Jewish country. Most of her class would not be allowed to live in such a country, not even dear, good Mrs Lohmann.

'No,' she said, 'I wish for a world where everyone can live together, Jews and other people. And I wish they would behave to each other the way they'd like others to behave to them.'

'I can't imagine a world like that,' whispered Rebekka.

Alice closed her eyes. She could imagine such a world. Some time, somewhere. She remembered again the lines on the gravestone of the drowned child: *Take me, Oh Love, to thee – ever thy child to be, till the day dawns.*

Then she fell asleep.

19

There was the window again, that huge window, and there was Alice, in the hall, running towards the window. It opened all by itself. Alice hopped on to the windowsill, opened her arms and flew down to the sea below. An azure-blue sea with a slightly crooked horizon: her birthday present from Grandfather, with a wavy pattern, like Grandmother's knitting, and a design of arcs of white foam. She circled above the shore, let herself be lifted by the air currents, sank when the wind dropped – the wonderfully warm, scented, delicate summer breeze.

From below Trudi was waving to her, and the rest of her class were there too. They were just walking across the dunes to the beach, and right at the back of the little crowd walked nice Mr Happel, who had always praised her drawings. There was the blonde woman too, in a green bathing-suit, sitting on a towel, watching her baby crawling in the sand and waving to the curly-headed child playing at the edge of a pool. The entire Maibaum family waded out of the sea in a long row, hand in hand, the youngest in the middle. And the three Silbermann girls stood by the kiosk, lapping up ice-creams.

On the waves, idly rising and falling, lay a boat in which Aaron and Samuel were fishing. Ruth and her children had built a beautiful sand-castle and were playing cards inside it, Struppi lying contentedly with them. The singer was walking beside the water, her head back, a silk scarf fluttering and her Persian coat slung over her left shoulder. And Paul, cheerful Paul, had already raised his hands: Punch and the magician. And her old class-mates, Trudi at their head, were rushing up to gather round him in a semicircle.

What a peaceful world.

But where were Mummy and Daddy and her grandparents? Alice, the seagull, swung away from the sea and flew inland, over the yacht harbour with all its gaily coloured boats. Before her lay the white town, full of arches and towers and many bay windows, with brilliant sunshades and sunroofs, set one above the other on the slope and encircled by gardens full of flowers. And there, under palm trees, among hibiscus bushes, at the round, white table of a pavement café – there were Mummy and Daddy, holding hands. And opposite them sat her grandparents, beckoning to Alice. Grandmother pointed to an empty chair between herself and Mummy, and Alice landed on it, light as a feather.

So now she was sitting on a wrought-iron chair, licking at the ice-cream in front of her, and surrounded by love and tenderness. Grandmother stroked her arm, Mummy kissed her long, loose hair, which fluttered in the wind, Grandfather showed her a velvety, shimmering butterfly, swinging on a hibiscus flower, and Daddy winked at her as he paid the bill. Then they walked into the town together, climbed up the winding steps, and strolled on, along pathways flecked with light and shade. At last they were back in the hall with the big window, below which the sea now stretched to the horizon, with a still wider sky above it: Nice, the South of France.

But here was Mrs Lohmann, grown to giant size, almost

filling the hall, and whispering, with fear in her eyes, 'The house still smells so strongly of coffee, Mrs Dubsky . . .'

Fierce sounds tore Alice from her sleep. For a moment she did not know where she was. What was this dark space? Who were these people sitting and lying on the floor? Why were they crying and shrieking like that? And what was that lying beside her, under the clothes?

She got up and turned, and there in front of her, by the light of a torch, she saw a stout young man with a bottle in his fist, flailing his arms about.

Now she knew where she was and who this young man was: Ernstl Herschel. He looked terrifying. Spittle was running from the corners of his mouth and dribbling from his chin. He was making sounds that reminded Alice of a dog growling.

Mr Ehrlich had also jumped up and was standing in front of Ernstl with clenched fists, Samuel beside him. What had happened? Had Ernstl tried to take Samuel's bottle away from him again? Or had the agonizing situation made him attack Mr Ehrlich?

Ernstl's sisters were wailing: people should leave it to them to calm their brother down. He was just excited. Nothing here was the way it was at home, and in any case he was still in pain after falling out of the truck.

'He's a madman!' shouted Mr Ehrlich. 'He's a danger to us all!'

Now Mr Blum was trying to calm Mr Ehrlich down, while the three Herschel sisters busied themselves with Ernstl. They stroked him, led him over to a rucksack, pushed him gently down on it and gave him a biscuit to eat. Suddenly he was in darkness; the torch that someone had directed at him was now swinging on its cord again and shining down on where Sarah Wormser must be lying.

'Turn the light on, Selma,' Alice heard Ernstl snivel. 'Now! Now! Want to go home.'

'We're on our way home, Ernstl,' said a woman's voice. 'Here we are in the train now. You know that.'

'Light!' he shouted.

'It's wartime, Ernstl. It always has to be dark like this in the trains, so that the bomber pilots don't see us.'

Brrm-brrmm, went Ernstl, moving his hand through the air like an aeroplane. Alice could see the outlines in the darkness.

'Go to sleep now,' said two women's voices at once. And then one of them went on, 'Be a good boy and shut your eyes.'

They leaned him against the wall.

The old Cohns tried to move further away from Ernstl, but everyone was sitting much closer together than at the beginning of the journey. The excrement had spread still further, and when Mr Blum stood up and shone his torch into the corner there were cries of shock.

'If the journey goes on much longer, we shall drown in it,' said a man's voice. Alice thought it was Mr Maibaum.

'We shall have to build a dam round it,' said the singer. 'Why don't you do something, you men?'

'We've got plenty of hands,' said Mr Blum, 'but no sand and no stones.'

Now everyone was talking at once. One thought it was simply a matter of standing all the cases in a row, but another objected that most of them were made of cardboard and would give way. A third thought the journey would soon be over. In the darkness Alice could not always make out which voices belonged to whom. The trench-coat woman recommended at least wiping up the longest tongues of muck, but when Mr Blum asked who could let them have paper or cloth for the purpose no one spoke, not even the trench-coat woman herself.

Suddenly there was a scream from the corner where Sarah Wormser lay.

'Yes,' cried Ruth, 'Yes! Push, Sarah, push! It's coming, It's coming! Give us a light!'

The constantly spreading brown mush was forgotten. Ernstl was forgotten. Another torch shone out in the corner. Alice was suddenly wide awake. She jumped up and craned her neck.

'Yes,' Mrs Herz was now loudly encouraging the labouring woman. 'Push! Push, Push!'

Between the black silhouettes, Alice could see the pale, naked body of the young woman. Mrs Silbermann pushed her daughters' heads down, and when the eldest tried to resist, Alice saw her mother box her ears.

'And you, you sit down!' shouted Mrs Silbermann angrily to Alice. When Alice stayed on her feet, Mrs Silbermann shouted, her voice cracking, 'Someone do something about that child!' But no one was listening to her.

Rebekka could not get up because her brothers' heads were still in her lap, and they were sleeping deeply.

'Is it happening?' she asked Alice, who shook her head.

'Let's hope it goes well,' sighed Mrs Cohn, now crouching with her husband under the grating beside the blonde woman.

Sarah's husband was kneeling by his wife's head, holding her hands and leaning over her. Alice heard him talking to her, softly and calmly. She could not understand what he was saying, but now and then she replied from a distorted face, 'Yes. Yes. Me you too, Willi. Yes . . .'

Another scream, and Alice saw the little head appear between Sarah's legs and Ruth's hands pulling gently. Then she saw blood. There was silence in the truck. Not even the youngest children made a sound. The blonde woman's baby was asleep.

'It's there,' Alice whispered to Rebekka.

'We have a son, Sarah,' said Mr Wormser, kissing his wife on the forehead.

Mrs Herz held up the child, which had started bawling. What a lot of blood there was all over it!

So this was a birth. This was the way she too had come into the world, naked and bathed in blood. Mummy and Daddy had come into the world like this, and her grandparents. And Mummy would certainly have screamed like that when she, Alice, came into the world. What a miracle!

20

•••

Alice was still standing in a trance. A blanket was spread over Sarah's body and legs and Ruth was cleaning the baby up with a damp cloth.

'We should really be singing a hosanna now,' said the singer.

White baby clothes were ready in the Wormsers' luggage. The child was dressed, his nappy put on, and now he looked as tiny babies always look: sweet. There was no more blood to be seen and he even had a thick, dark fuzz of hair on his small head.

Alice secretly wished she might take him in her arms and rock him to and fro. A real, live baby had been born here, here in this dark, stinking truck! If Grandfather and Paul had still been alive, with the men who had escaped, there would now have been fifty of them.

Mrs Herz laid the baby on Sarah's breast. 'That's just how my Max looked, just like that,' she said dreamily.

With a weak smile, Sarah stroked the baby's head and tucked her finger into the tiny fist.

'Have you got a bit of coffee left?' Ruth asked Alice. 'Sarah did well, and now she needs strength.'

Alice nodded, half-filled the screw-on top and handed it over. Torches lit it on its way as it passed carefully from hand to hand. Not a drop was lost. Everyone fell silent, following it with respectful eyes, as if it were a treasure. Willi Wormser raised his wife's head and supported her while she drank the coffee, which had been cold for a long time now, the coffee Grandmother had prepared on the last evening before their departure. All eyes were on Sarah. Alice could not imagine that there was anyone in the truck who would begrudge Sarah the coffee.

She sniffed at the open Thermos flask, breathing in the scent of coffee. The scent of home. And yet it was also the smell of fear. Every evening Grandmother had placed the Thermos full of hot, fresh coffee in the holdall, only to take it out again the next morning and fill the breakfast cups from it. What fear Mummy, Daddy and her grand-parents must have suffered every night. All the same, they had been able to act out a normal life for Alice in the day-time, and she, Alice, had had no suspicion of all that tension. She had nagged and fidgeted and made life difficult for the grown-ups. Oh, Grandmother. Wherever she was – if only she could sense in some way how much Alice loved her!

Then the new-born baby was tucked into an empty travel bag. His parents seemed to have thought of everything before they left. The bag had little pillows inside it.

'I ought to have brought a bag like that,' Alice heard the blonde woman say. 'But who has any idea what is going to happen to them?'

The coffee top came back empty, and even the torches, including Alice's, made their way back to their owners. Mr Wormser called out a thank-you to Alice, nodded and smiled all round and put his raised hands together in a gesture of thanks.

'What's his name to be?' called the trench-coat man.

Mr Wormser was embarrassed. 'She wants him to be called Willi,' he said.

'Long live Willi Wormser!' cried the trench-coat man.

There was muted applause; people were tired. Rebekka seemed the most tired of all. She groaned and stretched the upper part of her body to left and right, trying not to disturb her two brothers. 'I can't sit here any longer,' she whispered to Alice. 'I'm quite stiff.'

Ruth had not yet returned to her place and Mrs Herz was also still attending to Sarah. Towels were needed – Sarah was bleeding badly – but who would have brought towels on a journey?

When the blonde woman was asked for nappies she shook her head. She had only two clean ones left in her own luggage. Why not use some of the baby's? But all but three of the nappies from the Wormsers' luggage had been used for the birth.

Ruth got Rebekka to give her a towel from their rucksack and Mrs Herz brought one out of her luggage as well. 'This belongs to Max, and he is not here,' she said.

Alice rummaged round and got three towels out of her bag, and two little handkerchiefs with lace edging. Ruth handed them all over except for the third towel, which she returned to Alice. 'You'll be needing that yourself,' she said, and then called to Mrs Cohn, 'Couldn't you let us have your lovely big tablecloth –'

'The cross-stitched tablecloth?' cried the old woman, shocked. 'God save us, can you imagine how long it took me to embroider that?'

'All right,' sighed Ruth, 'I only asked.'

'Ruth,' Rebekka called wearily, 'please come! I can't go on.'

'In a moment, child,' Ruth called back.

At last Sarah's bleeding seemed to have been stemmed. The women washed her, covered her over again and left her to sleep. It was dark and silent in her corner. On the other hand, in the opposite corner, where the lavatory was, there was much lively coming and going. Waves of stench filled the room.

'Diarrhoea,' said one of the Maibaums. 'I'm sure of it . . .'

'The dirty water from the buckets,' groaned someone as he squatted. 'And I'm still so thirsty.' Alice thought she recognized Mr Grün's voice.

Ruth returned to her place and handed her the torch. 'Thank you, Alice. That was the best torch,' she said. 'Without it, everything might have gone quite differently . . .'

Alice felt herself go red.

Ruth pushed her way between the luggage and the children, lifted her sons' heads from Rebekka's lap on to her own, and Rebekka rolled over and fell asleep instantly.

Alice was much too excited to sleep. She directed the beam of the torch, now much weaker than during the birth, on to the two dead bodies, arranged their clothing and touched Paul's hand. It was cold and stiff.

'Is that why you can't sleep, Alice?' whispered Ruth. 'Perhaps you should sit somewhere else?'

No, Alice wanted to stay where she was. These two dead bodies belonged to her. She would stay with them until they were buried. Her thoughts shifted to the baby. She herself wanted to have at least six children later on, even if each birth made her cry out with pain. Six children – they could be boys or girls. If she had three boys and three girls, the girls would have Mummy's and Grandmother's names and the youngest would be Trudi. The boys would be called after Daddy and Grandfather, and the youngest Paul. And the man she married would look like Paul and be as nice with children as he was. That would be a wonderful family! They would go back to live on the upper floors of the white house, from which you could see the whole town. Her children would play in the garden, under the big trees, and her husband would build them a tree house.

And in the holidays they would all go to Nice.

She had been five when they went to Nice, but she could still remember their compartment on the train: a first-class sleeper. They had always travelled first class, even on the short journey to see Uncle Ludwig and Aunt Irene.

Alice remembered red velvet and elegant curtains at the windows. In the morning the soft beds turned into seats and then Daddy rang for a waiter and ordered breakfast, while her grandparents joined them from the next compartment. There had been pictures on the walls. She could still see one of them clearly: a wedding party, seated before a country inn. Grandfather had told her that they were having a 'wedding breakfast'. The picture was in a frame carved to represent a wreath of grapes, vine leaves and spiral tendrils.

Since then, the picture had come into her mind whenever she thought about a wedding. She imagined her own wedding like that one: all the guests sitting round a big table in front of an inn in the country and her husband and herself in the middle; music playing, plenty of delicacies on the table, everyone laughing and raising their glasses . . .

Alice stood up. Now it was her turn, however much she loathed that corner; but what could she do? Her stomach was rumbling loudly. Bull-neck had taken her roll of paper and now he had gone.

She shone her torch into the holdall and rummaged again, discovering a folder of Grandfather's papers, which must be very important. There were also two photograph albums and a little book: *Faust* by Goethe.

'Do stop your fidgeting!' hissed Bull-neck's girlfriend.

'Even if you can't get to sleep, you might at least give others a chance.'

Alice switched off the torch, waited a moment and then took from her coat pocket the three letters, written with love – letters which were nevertheless false. Now her need was really urgent. Taking the torch, she reached the corner just in time. She had diarrhoea – liquid ran out in a stream so that she could not avoid stepping in it. The first letter crackled in her hand. Then the second. Then the third. It was pointless to unfold them. They were so tattered that they almost fell to pieces in her hands.

'Hurry up,' came a groan.

Alice did her best. For a moment she found herself wondering what a genuine letter from her parents would be like, if they knew where she was now. An honest letter. Perhaps it would say:

Dear Alice,
Be brave. Make the best of what is happening. Don't give up. Try to sell your life as dearly as possible. Never forget that they can soil you only on the outside, and don't forget that you are loved.

Mummy and Daddy

'I can't stay here,' wailed Mrs Herz.

'Move across! Move closer together!'

When Alice returned to her place she realized that the longest tongue had already reached Ruth's rucksack and was now only about three hands' breadths from Paul's feet. With her bag she moved a little further to the right and pushed the rucksack out of the mess without waking Ruth.

21

•••

Rat-tat-tat, rat-tat-tat. Alice thought of the three men who had escaped: Moustache, Bull-neck and Max. Three men, unarmed, without provisions, maps or even a covering for the night. All three had leaped from the train without their coats. They must be freezing now it was cold. Perhaps they were huddled – if they were still alive – close together in a cattle barn? A haystack? A thicket? In any case, in some strange place far from home, full of fear and desperately hungry. So she, Alice, here in the stinking truck, sheltered among the others, was better off after all.

Only a little while ago in the basement, she had read a novel about an escape which took place in the days when noblemen carried daggers. A young nobleman in the service of a foreign ruler had escaped from his executioners and made his way by night to his homeland. A handsome, well-dressed man who always had money in his pocket. Wherever he sought shelter he was taken in, women fell at his feet and wept for him. Good luck and quick wits helped him out of every difficult situation and of course he could speak all the necessary foreign languages.

The three men from the truck could probably speak a few phrases of English at best, but where they were that would not help either. England and America – as Alice knew – were far away, and the young men were not noblemen with plenty of money in their pockets. Above all, there was no point in their making their way home – that was the most dangerous place of all. Non-Jews would certainly be strictly forbidden to hide Jews, and anyone who did so, like Mrs Lohmann, would also risk being transported in a train like this.

Poor men. What use was it to them to be able to smell water, woods and wild flowers? Their chances of survival were slim.

Alice wondered what it would be like to be dead. Was it true that you would be completely happy, as Ruth had said? She remembered how, soon after Prussi's death, she had asked Mr Weinrich, the grumpy gardener, what he thought. He was just moving some primulas and other plants to a border. Without stopping what he was doing, Mr Weinrich suddenly became quite talkative: 'If you ask me – I don't believe a word of all that nonsense about heaven and hell and numbered seats under God's throne. That's just something the parsons tell us to make us put up with everything here and look forward to being "over there". But you wouldn't understand that yet, girl.'

Alice had run after him, because it was true that she had scarcely understood a word he said. Only the numbered seats. She had wanted to know all about it, but he had been stubbornly silent. To her question as to whether it was beautiful there, he had answered gruffly, 'What's beautiful? Remember what it was like when you were still inside your mother, then you'll know.'

Alice understood that least of all. All she could make of his words was that he had meant 'in your mother's arms'.

In Mummy's arms? Alice had a vague memory of the day when the new swing was put up in the garden. The supports still smelled of creosote, and there was a thick bed of sand under the swing. Daddy had put Alice on the swing and pushed her gently to and fro. Her grandparents and Mummy had watched and called to her, 'Don't be afraid, Mousie, nothing's going to happen to you!' But she had screamed with fear, feeling everything spinning around her. Her feet did not reach the ground and she clung fiercely to the ropes.

The grown-ups had burst out laughing. Then Mummy had stopped the swing, sat in it herself and taken Alice on her lap. Daddy had pushed them both carefully to and fro.

Alice had been held safely in her mother's arms. The up and down, to and fro, with no ground beneath her feet had suddenly become so beautiful, so truly wonderful.

But the gardener had not meant 'in Mummy's arms', she knew that now. He had meant precisely what he said: *inside your mother.*

Alice heard someone crying and just after that she heard the blonde woman whisper, 'I think he's ill. He's breathing much too fast.' Someone, perhaps Mrs Herz, replied, so softly that Alice could not hear what she was saying. Then the blonde woman spoke again: 'Such a sweet child, too.' And after a pause, quite pitifully, 'They can't do that to us . . .'

Alice wanted to know what was going on. Were they talking about Benni, the curly-haired boy, or the baby? She moved a little closer to the blonde on her knees and then noticed that her knees were moving through something cold and wet. In a panic she switched on her torch and directed it at the floor. She was kneeling right in the revolting mess.

With a scream she fled to Grandfather's legs, where she crouched, her back to the sliding-door, pointed the torch at her filthy knees and screamed and screamed. Other torches went on. 'Quiet!' someone called angrily. The blonde's baby began to cry, and Benni and the youngest Maibaum wailed.

'Pull yourself together, Alice,' said Ruth harshly, and, pushing the sleeping boys to one side, she sat down on Alice's holdall and took Alice on her lap.

Here, between Ruth's breasts and her folded knees, Alice came to her senses again. Here she felt safe.

To be able to sit on someone's lap again – she would not have dared to dream of it. She heard Mr Blum's voice behind her, turned her head and saw him clambering over seated people and luggage to the corner.

'Yes,' he said, 'something's got to be done here.'

Mr Silbermann and Mr Maibaum stood up as well to talk it over with Mr Blum. Mrs Maibaum joined them. For a time she just listened, then she went into action. 'Come on, all you who haven't given anything yet!' she cried, snatching the torch from Mr Blum and shining it on the seated people. 'Here we sit, all in the same boat, it couldn't be worse!' She beckoned the Grüns and the Herschels.

From the safety of Ruth's lap, Alice observed what happened next. At first the Grüns did not want to move. He claimed a headache, she said she was indisposed. And then the two little girls – they would wake up, become restless, not understand what was going on.

'I've got children too,' said Mrs Maibaum. 'As if there was anything worse than what we've had to tell them these past days!'

Mr Grün let himself be talked round at last. No, Mr Blum said, the Herschel sisters should be left in peace, otherwise Ernstl would rebel again. They had enough trouble dealing with him.

'But you,' cried Mrs Maibaum, pointing to the singer. 'You're not too high and mighty to shit – or are you?'

The singer pretended not to hear.

'Then next time you'll shit in your own suitcase, you can depend on it!' scolded Mrs Maibaum.

She beckoned to Mrs Silbermann, and even the trench-coat pair stood up before Mrs Maibaum ordered them to. Their faces dark, as if they meant vengeance, the trench-coat man and Mr Grün rolled up their sleeves. Mother Maibaum took the torch from Mr Blum and lit up all the corners where light was needed. From the Wormsers' corner she demanded the bloody towels and with Mrs Grün's help twisted them into a rope. Samuel was given the torch to hold and had to keep it shining on their hands. Alice understood: they were going to build a dam which would both absorb and hold back the mess.

'Any unwanted bits and pieces over here!' cried Mrs Maibaum. 'They won't be lost, only dirty. Somewhere there's bound to be water again . . .'

Light fell through the gratings and moved across the seated people. Alice saw that many eyes were closed.

'Don't pretend you're asleep,' said Mrs Maibaum loudly. 'And anyone who doesn't give something will have to move closer to the muck – right, Mr Blum?'

Mrs Maibaum stood like a monument between the shifting lights. In the semi-darkness Alice could see only the outline of her body, but on the morning before the departure she had been standing near the Maibaums and had had plenty of time to look at her: the frayed dress, the shabby blouse, the fiercely combed-back hair, the thick, sturdy neck.

The blonde woman handed a dirty nappy over to Mother Maibaum and Alice threw over her cap and scarf. It was summertime, after all. Why worry about next winter now? She asked Ruth to get up, so that she could hand over Grandfather's and Grandmother's underclothes and socks and stockings. Now the big holdall was quite limp. Only the bottom was still covered.

'Just look at that child!' cried Mrs Maibaum.

Even the Herschels passed something across the truck and the Maibaum grandmother gave up a shawl. The red-cheeked woman threw a man's jacket to Mrs Maibaum and Mr Ehrlich gave up a waistcoat.

'It doesn't matter now,' said Mrs Herz, and allowed herself to be parted from her son's clothes. After that she blew her nose for a long time.

'He was an informer,' Ruth whispered to Alice. 'He had a couple who were in hiding on his conscience. That's why his mother didn't want anything more to do with him. They were not speaking to each other. And then it was his turn after all.'

'Give us a light over here, Alice,' called the blonde woman. Beside her, under the grating, stood Paul's rucksack. By the light of the torch, now very weak, she pulled out all the pieces of clothing and threw them to the trench-coat woman. Under the other grating Mrs Grün emptied Moustache's case, and by now the rest of the helpers were there, damming the tongues of muck and shoving them back towards the corner.

'Can you manage on your own now?' asked Ruth. Alice nodded and Ruth went to her children. Alice sat in the holdall with her knees pulled up. When she shone the light into the corner after a time there were no more tongues to be seen and the lumpy mess had been dammed up behind articles of every shape and size.

'There,' said Mrs Maibaum, wiping her hands on a blood-spattered cloth, which she then twisted into a sausage and laid on the top of the dam. 'And no one is to tread on the dam. It is a masterpiece. Nobody's going to break *that* down very fast!'

The train rumbled over points in the line. Light came through the gratings and Mr Blum spied through Moustache's grating. 'Oppeln,' he said.

Alice had never heard the name Oppeln. Were they already in the east?

The train slowed down and stopped. To judge by the lights, they must be in a station. Alice held her breath. Was the train finally going to stop here?

The answer came from Mr Blum: 'We have stopped at the goods platform!'

Samuel, now also at the grating, reported that Red Cross nurses were hurrying towards the engine, where presumably the guards had their own compartment. They were carrying a big stewpan, he said.

'If *they* are being given something to eat now,' Alice heard the blonde woman say, 'might we get something too?'

From the other trucks they heard again the cry of 'Water!' Through the grating Samuel shouted to somebody, 'We have a new-born baby and the mother in here. We need a doctor! And we've got two dead bodies in the truck!'

Mr Blum shouted too, with a few of the others. After a time they stopped. 'There's no point,' sighed Mr Blum.

'You're all filth, the lot of you out there!' screamed the blonde woman. 'How many children have you already got on your conscience?'

No one opened the sliding-door. No men's voices roared outside. But then it seemed that someone must be walking past the truck, because Mr Blum called through the grating, 'Please – we have small children in here. We need water for them at least . . .'

'Quiet in there!' was the answer. 'You'll be there soon – maybe sooner than you'd like.'

'Where?' asked Mr Blum and Samuel at once. And when

no one answered them, they shouted, now in another direction, 'Where are we going?'

Everyone in the truck listened with them.

'He didn't even turn round,' said Samuel furiously. 'Just making out he's deaf.'

'We're used to that from them,' said Mr Ehrlich.

'But it wasn't one of the guards,' said Samuel. 'It was a railway man. A pointsman or something!'

After a time they heard women's voices nearby. Something clattered. 'The nurses are coming back,' Samuel reported. 'The pot is empty.'

Aaron also tried to look through the grating, but he could not reach it.

'What about us?' shouted the blonde woman. 'When do we get something to eat?'

After barely half an hour the train moved off again.

'God help us,' said someone.

22

•••

'You'll be there soon,' one of the guards had told them. Good news – or not? It depended where 'there' was. And what had the phrase 'maybe sooner than you'd like' meant? Alice tried to picture a camp. Was it a big place with a fence round it? But there must be houses there too, with bedrooms and bathrooms and lavatories. Perhaps the camp was already full up? Would they have to do hard work? Somewhere she was bound to find room for the holdall and rucksack and at least everyone would be given a mattress to sleep on. She did not need anything else, and she was looking forward to the work.

Then she thought about Max's story. She could not get it out of her mind. Was it *Max* who had betrayed their basement hiding-place? But if so, would he have been taken away together with his victims? And in any case, how could he have known that the Dubskys were living in – No. The suspicion seemed absurd.

Suddenly she remembered Mr Weinrich, the gardener. Had he been the one? When he moved out of the basement, he was already seventy-one and had looked after the garden painstakingly for decades. He would certainly never have imagined doing anything but look after it until he died, which also meant living in the basement until he died. Alice knew that he had been alone, without friends or relations.

And then, after so many years together, Grandfather had dismissed him. He would certainly never have told him that they, the Dubskys, were going to move into that tiny basement flat themselves. Perhaps Grandfather had talked about emigration. And about the house being sold.

Alice had seen Mr Weinrich crying. He had blown his nose surreptitiously again and again as he raked up the leaves. She had asked him why he was crying and he had hastily wiped his eyes and said he was not crying, that his eyes were just running a little because of the wind.

Soon after that he had gone – gone without a word. Perhaps he had sometimes walked secretly round the house and seen the garden gradually becoming overgrown. Might he have kept a key to the garden gate when he left? Mr Weinrich had always been responsible for the garden gate. But if he was the informer, why had he not betrayed them for two years? No, it was all nonsense. Mr Weinrich was grumpy, but not spiteful.

Suddenly Alice felt desperately thirsty. There was a little coffee left. She emptied out the Thermos flask to the very last drop. In the light of her torch, which she was holding under her chin, that drop shimmered for a long time before it fell. She directed the light into the cup; it was barely half full. She would be drinking Grandmother's coffee for the last time, perhaps the last ever. It shone blackly in the cup – like the water in a deep well. Unfathomable. Mysterious.

'Stop your fidgeting or I'll belt you!' scolded the red-cheeked woman.

Alice tried to shade the light. She moved the torch to and fro and when the beam fell on her face, her reflection appeared in the cup against a black ground. Two eyes, a nose, a mouth – scarcely recognizable to Alice. She stared, fascinated, at her own face. How often had she looked at herself in the mirror, trying different hairstyles and clothes, laughing and grimacing. That bright Alice against a green and white patterned curtain she knew inside out, whether sitting or standing, turning this way or that.

But this Alice, scarcely visible in the depths of the well, nothing but eyes, mouth and nose – this Alice was new to her.

Alice, Jewess, also known as pest. No one had asked her before she was born if she wanted to be Jewish. She gave her frowning brows, her compressed lips, a hostile stare. Did that face look evil? Or was it just the way she was holding the torch?

'Now that's enough!' shouted the red-cheeked woman furiously, suddenly leaning forward and aiming a blow at Alice, who succeeded in ducking just in time so that the blow missed her head. She switched off the torch. Now the woman could see her only as a dark shadow, and Alice herself could see almost nothing – neither the cup nor the coffee, neither the round well nor the black depths with the dark face reflected in them.

But it was important that that face should cease to exist. It was still in the cup – in the well. She had only to switch the torch on again to convince herself that it was still there.

She must get rid of it. So she raised the cup and drank. After that she stopped thinking altogether and heard only the rattle of the wheels. Some time later – she had no idea how long it was – in spite of the coffee she was overcome by such leaden tiredness that she pushed the torch into her rucksack and rolled up in the holdall. She pulled her knees up to her chin, pressed her hands, clenched into fists, against her cheeks and temples, and closed her eyes.

A very, very distant memory brushed her mind. Not a

nice memory. It conjured up the fear that Alice had sensed at that time – she could not have been much more than three years old, four at most – when she had tried to strike a match, just as cook always did by the stove. But this time she had been alone in the room and suddenly, after the third or fourth stroke against the rough side of the box, a flame had flared up, a bright, hot fire, which seemed huge to the little girl. For a fraction of a second she had stared into the flickering light, bursting with pride: she alone had made this fire! But what now? The flame was eating its way along the wood towards her fingers and you could not simply drop fire! Alice began to cry, but did not let go of the match.

Then cook had burst in through one door and Grandfather through the other. He had blown out the flame and taken Alice in his arms and rocked her. Then everything was all right again.

Alice was awakened by a scream. It came from the trench-coat woman, who was completely beside herself. 'Who trod on the dam? It's running out in all directions!'

The people in the truck went into action. Those who were closest to the lavatory corner tried to get to a safe place. Children cried. The Herschel sisters wept. Alice gradually realized what had happened. The Herschels had led Ernstl – probably in darkness – to the corner and told him to squat. But the lavatory at home was quite different; he must have refused, pushing them away, and that was when it had happened. Streams were trickling from the corner in all directions.

Alice felt safe in her holdall, as if she were in a boat. And without concerning herself with the others' cries and the feverish wiping up, she dozed off again.

Something else swam to the surface of her mind, more distant than the fire memory, vaguer – more of a sensation than an event. She was lying in warm water, closely held against someone, perhaps Daddy, perhaps Mummy. Then she was lifted out of the warmth and wrapped in something, probably a towel. Alice was still just a baby. She could see faces above her and she struggled and cried. It had been so lovely in the warm water, and her longing to return to the warmth, to the familiar closeness of a beloved human being, became overwhelming – so great that Alice let herself be carried off into a deep, dreamless sleep, which swathed her in warm redness.

When she woke up, light was already dawning through the gratings. Her first thought was for the Wormsers. Mr Wormser had the baby's carrying bag on his lap. Sarah was still asleep.

Alice saw that the dam had been replaced round the corner. Everything was calm and peaceful in the truck now. No one was crying; no one was scolding. Most people were asleep. Mrs Herz had the baby on her lap; the blonde woman sighed in her sleep, her head resting on Mrs Herz's shoulder. The curly-haired child slept on the floor between their outspread legs. The Herschel sisters looked crumpled and dishevelled. Between them Ernstl snored, plump as a maggot. The Herschels had always protected Ernstl from other people, Alice had heard Mrs Herz telling the blonde woman. No one had dreamed that things were so difficult.

The Maibaum clan was snoring, except for the two daughters, who were sitting up, putting on make-up in front of a tiny mirror which they held up to their faces in turn.

The singer was a wretched sight. In her sleep she had fallen from her case on to the dirty floor. Her turban was awry, her dress had hitched up and left her petticoat and knickers open to view.

Ruth woke up, rose cautiously and reached for the roll of paper in the outside pocket of her rucksack. Alice saw her go over to the corner and squat, no longer finding this situation at all embarrassing. When she came back she smiled at Alice and fell asleep again.

Then the sleepy faces of Ida and Ilse popped up out of the hilly landscape of bodies and luggage. Someone complained of thirst; paper rustled; someone farted.

Mr Silbermann and Mr Grün got up at the same time, stepped over the luggage and met at the peeing crack. Each wanted the other to go first and so they argued for a while until at last Mr Silbermann stepped up to the crack. Alice had heard from Rebekka that Mr Silbermann was a tax consultant – whatever that was.

Someone was murmuring. Several people were murmuring at once. It sounded as if they were praying, but if so, to whom? Alice remembered the last two lines of 'A Child's Prayer in Winter', which she had learned in Class Two. It had been in their reading book and the last two lines had run: '*All of those who dream in darkness, shelter softly with Thy snow.*' She could scarcely have thought of anything more unsuitable now, in August. But it did her good to think of snow. An endless stretch of cold and quietness. A landscape of crystals of wondrous purity.

To be clean again, without thirst.

Alice had a feeling in her stomach. It was very painful, but not like the stomach pains before diarrhoea. These new pains were more unpleasant, almost alarming. But should she wake up Ruth for that? Ruth had earned a couple of hours' sleep – and the stomach pain was bearable, after all.

God. Did he exist or not? And if so, what had he to do with this journey?

Alice shivered, feeling extraordinarily alone.

Grandfather, dear Grandfather. If he were still alive, he would draw her to him and hug her and wipe away her tears. She leaned over him, anxious at least to see him – his big nose and bushy eyebrows, his whole well-loved face.

But when she raised the corner of Grandmother's dress, which she had spread over his head, a strange face appeared. Of course his big nose was still there, and his heavy eyebrows, but it was not Grandfather's face. A stranger lay there, someone she had never met. His upper lip was pulled back a little, his teeth shining beneath it. The gold tooth she knew so well was there too, but in a stranger's mouth.

Alice no longer had the courage to look at Paul again. Let him remain covered; then he at least was still as she had known him – young and handsome as a prince.

23

•••

Alice started. Had she nodded off again? Even the two Maibaum daughters seemed to be asleep. It was still quite quiet in the truck.

She stood up and looked around at the sleepers. She was the only one on her feet, the only one awake, and yet it was morning. A reddish shaft of light fell through the opposite grating: sunrise, another brilliant August day.

Then she heard the sound of brakes which by now she knew so well. Her whole body listened, and at last the sleepers were also woken up by the hissing of the brakes.

Questions tumbled over one another: 'Where are we?' 'Are we there?' Samuel jumped up and peered through his grating, Isolde crowding against him. 'Nothing to be seen,' he announced, 'only a couple of sheds and brick buildings.'

Then Samuel said, 'The place is called Auschwitz.'

Auschwitz? Alice looked across at Mr Blum, who pulled down the corners of his mouth and shrugged his shoulders.

How different the men looked now: unshaven, uncombed, with crumpled shirt collars and creased, stained trousers. And the women were no better: their clothes dirty and wrinkled, their hair tousled. Only the two Maibaum daughters and Isolde stood out, with their red lips, powdered cheeks and eyeshadow. Ilse and Ida cried. They wanted to look beautiful too; they had never been allowed to use make-up.

The truck was becoming very noisy. The children complained; Ernstl started crying and would not be silenced The trench-coat woman cursed when she discovered that her case was standing in the muck. The two Cohns wailed softly.

Suddenly there was a lot to do. The luggage was organized at high speed.

'Pack up, Alice!' cried Ruth. 'Get ready quickly, Ruben, David!'

'Yes, Ida, of course there will be a washroom in the camp.'

'Be quiet, Walter. We're there now and we'll get a drink.'

The train rumbled across some points, slowing down all the time. The men crowded to the gratings.

Mrs Maibaum gave one of her boys a resounding box on the ear, but Alice never knew why. Mr Ehrlich dusted his hat while the Trench-coats were busy trying to clean their cases. The red-cheeked woman beside Alice was on her feet, packing her rucksack, and Alice saw for the first time that she had a club foot.

'Listen, Alice,' called out the blonde woman, an undertone of desperation in her voice, 'you've got your rucksack for your things. Couldn't you leave me the heavy holdall – for my Lotti?'

Alice nodded, stooped and began to pull the remaining bits and pieces out of the holdall.

'Looks as if we're going through an archway,' said Samuel.

'Thanks, my girl,' said the blonde woman distractedly. 'Give it here, quick. We'll be there in a minute.'

Alice tipped the holdall upside-down. Everything left inside now fell on Paul's body. But something flat, large and unwieldy was stuck at the bottom of the bag: the family tree. Grandfather had packed it.

'Come on!' cried the blonde woman, panicking.

Alice handed the bag over to her, opened her rucksack and stuffed all her things in it: washing things, some underwear, socks, a nightdress, a second dress, a pair of gym shoes, the torch, all kinds of bits and pieces. And suddenly Mummy's jewel case was in her hand. Oh, Grandfather. He must have managed to stuff it in the bag at the last moment, because she had been playing with the necklaces and bracelets only the day before. She pushed the jewel case hastily into her coat pocket.

The train was stopping, with a horribly shrill, metallic screech. There was a rattling already at the opposite sliding-door, which was pushed open. Light flooded in, making the people in the truck blink. Then there was utter confusion. Suddenly everything was happening at breathtaking speed.

Men in striped clothing appeared in the door opening and roared something at the people in the truck. They lifted down the old Cohns, who did not know what was happening to them. Outside a loudspeaker boomed.

'Get out! Everyone out!' shouted the men in stripes.

'These belong to us, of course,' said Mrs Maibaum, giving her daughters a bucket each to hold. 'Or has anyone any objection? Buckets are always useful. Get out? Gladly! Whatever you say . . .'

The truck emptied. Suddenly there was so much room. Alice was astonished to see how much of the truck floor the muck had not reached. A striped man climbed in, lifted Sarah Wormser and passed her over to another standing below. Then he helped the Maibaum grandparents out of the truck.

'What about Grandfather and Paul!' cried Alice, pointing desperately at the dead bodies.

'They will be taken care of, child,' said the striped man.

Rebekka, David and Ruben were already on the platform, calling her. Ruth was in a hurry. A second striped man climbed into the truck.

'But I want to know where they will be buried,' sobbed Alice.

'You'll find out all about it, and today,' said the striped man solemnly. 'So now, out with you, girl.'

He took her under the armpits and handed her down to Ruth.

'You don't even know my name,' she cried in panic fear. 'How are you going to find me among all these people?'

'That's right,' said the striped man, who was already pulling Paul towards the opening. 'I had almost forgotten that. What is your name?'

'Alice Dubsky,' she said. 'Eleven years old, nearly twelve.'

'Alice in Wonderland,' said the striped man. 'That's easy to see. So, we'll tell you all about it, today. You can depend on it.'

Alice took a deep breath. That was arranged, then. The loudspeaker was still booming and, once outside, Alice could understand what it was saying: 'Leave all luggage. Women on one side! Men on the other!'

She stared back into the open truck, saw her grandfather lying there and could not bear to be parted from him. This was the last time she would see him. Next time she would be able to see only his grave.

'Come on!' urged Ruth, pulling Alice away.

All the luggage was lined up in front of the trucks; only Mrs Silbermann was clinging to her rucksack. 'My pills,' she clamoured. 'If Ilse gets an attack of asthma and we haven't got the luggage with us –'

'We can't simply leave our cases here,' Alice heard the trench-coat woman protesting. She turned round, ran a few steps back and looked into the truck again. Inside, the striped man was just pulling Grandfather towards the door opening. Alice burst into tears. Ruth tried to pull her away, but Alice resisted.

'He's dead, child,' said the striped man. 'He doesn't feel anything now. He's all right, believe me. Better than the rest of us.'

'Bury them side-by-side,' pleaded Alice. 'At least they know each other. They won't be so alone –'

'Shall be done, Alice,' said the striped man. 'Word of honour.'

'Women and children who cannot walk,' boomed the voice from the loudspeaker repeatedly, 'go to the vehicles waiting for them!'

Rebekka, Ruben and David had already gone ahead in the direction everyone was taking. People seemed to be gathering at the front, in an open space beside the train.

Ruth took Alice's rucksack and added it to her own luggage.

'Come on!' called Rebekka, beckoning impatiently.

Alice walked along the train, looking into each truck she passed. All of them stank; some of them were dripping brown mush. Dead bodies lay outside three trucks. She turned her head and looked the other way. There were three covered lorries. The blonde woman went straight over to one of them, the holdall in one hand, the curly-haired child holding the other, her rucksack on her back. What of the baby? It must be in the holdall. Behind her the old Cohns limped along, and in the lorry Alice recognized Mr Wormser with the little carrying bag in which the new-born baby lay. He spoke to one of the striped men, then disappeared inside the lorry, in which his wife was probably waiting. It was good that she could be driven; she was still too weak to walk without help.

A few metres away from the trucks stood uniformed men

with dogs. Somebody screamed. Alice looked this way and that. There was so much happening, all at the same time, she simply did not know where to look first. It was a child that was screaming, a little girl from another truck, wearing a bright blue dress. 'Mum! Mum!' she screamed, stumbling along beside the train. A striped man took her by the hand and led her to one of the lorries.

24

•••

The loudspeaker was silent now. Alice turned. The people who had been travelling in the trucks at the back had formed a long procession, blocking her view. She could not see if the striped men had already taken Paul and Grandfather out of the truck, but the men had promised to let her know today where they were buried. So it must be quite possible here to find one particular person among so many. And, it seemed, it must be possible to get all those many pieces of luggage, whether they had names on or not, back to their owners. Many things seemed to be possible here!

She kept on looking about her. Yes, Samuel had been right: the train had run under a great archway. It spanned the lines in the background, gleaming in the morning sun.

'Don't hang about like that,' said Ruth. 'We might miss something because of you . . .'

So many men in uniform. So many dogs. Why were they there? One man in stripes was standing in the opening of a truck. 'Where are we going now?' asked a woman with a child in her arms, walking ahead of Alice.

'To shower,' he said. 'And afterwards, to start with, hot coffee.'

Shower! Of course, that was more than necessary for all of them.

When they reached the open square they saw two groups, which were visibly growing: women and children on one side, men on the other. Alice saw a uniformed man cross over to the men's group and beckon to Aaron. 'That one's still a child,' he shouted.

'But I'm a widower,' she heard Mr Ehrlich call back. 'My boy won't have anyone to take care of him over there.'

'You'll be seeing each other in no time,' shouted the uniformed man, and Alice was surprised that his voice was quite friendly. He even clapped Aaron on the shoulder, said something to him and then pushed him towards the mothers and children.

'Come in with us,' Ruth called to him. He nodded with relief and came over.

'What did that man say to you?' asked Rebekka.

The words seemed to have stuck in Aaron's mind: 'You're not so small that you still need to hold Daddy's hand, boy . . .'

Now they were wedged into the huge crowd made up of women and children. Ruth tried to stay on the outside so that Aaron did not lose sight of his father and brother. Next to them were the Silbermanns without Mr Silbermann, and Mrs Grün and her two girls were close by – Mrs Grün, who had thrown all those letters from the train.

'If only I knew how they think they're going to arrange for the luggage later on,' said Mrs Silbermann.

A man in stripes pushed past them to a group walking a little ahead. Surely those were the hats of the three Herschel sisters and between them Ernstl, easy to see in his peaked cap. Why were they pressing round him so closely? Did they want to make him invisible? Were they trying to hide him from somebody? At that moment the man in stripes took him by the arm and tried to pull him out of the little press of women – probably because he should have been on the other side.

But Ernstl was struggling. 'No!' cried the sisters, 'he needs us!' And, 'He's just like a child!'

The other women squeezed quickly past the group, and two more uniformed men came up and pushed the sisters away. They boxed Ernstl's ears, seized him by the arms and dragged him over to the men's side. Ernstl shouted desperately, 'Lina! Selma! Edith!' The men stepped back, startled, from the uniformed men and Ernstl, who vanished in the crowd. Alice heard Ernstl give one last screech, before the sisters' shrill, lamenting cries drowned all other sounds: 'Ernstl! Ernstl!'

'Move on,' a man in stripes shouted at Ruth and the children.

The procession was in order again, the gap closed.

'What will they do with him now, Ruth?' asked David, very upset.

'I don't know, David,' said Ruth quietly.

'Where are they taking him?'

'I don't know, I don't know –'

Alice's head thudded. There was a rushing in her ears and her knees grew weak. And this pain in her stomach!

They were approaching a group of uniformed men, visible between the shoulders of the people walking in front of them. Among them was an older man in civilian clothes, wearing a long, dark coat. It was like Grandfather's – double-breasted, with slanting pockets.

A thought shot through Alice's mind. 'The coat is still in the truck!' she cried. 'Grandfather's coat, the one Mrs Wormser was lying on.'

She let go of Ruth and tried to push her way back through the crowd that was building up behind them, but Ruth held on to her. 'Forget it,' she said. 'It's covered with blood, and they certainly won't let you go back to the truck.'

Between them and the group of uniformed men there were now only the Maibaums, the trench-coat woman, the singer and the red-cheeked woman with the club foot. The central figure was a tall, slim man, with braid and piping on his uniform – an officer. He flicked a casual, elegant hand: the trench-coat woman to the right, the red-cheeked woman and the singer to the left, the Maibaum daughters to the right, Mrs Maibaum with her little boy, the grandmother and the youngest, in her arms, to the left.

And now it was their turn – Ruth with the boys and Rebekka, together with Aaron and herself, all to the left. When Alice looked round, she saw that Mrs Grün with her two little girls was following them. After that there was a brief hold-up, because Ida had been waved to the left and Isolde, Ilse and their mother to the right. But Mrs Silbermann clutched Ida and would not be parted from her. The officer smiled, as though he understood, and sent all four of them to the left.

'Come on, Alice,' Ruth commanded. 'We've got no time to stand here staring.'

'Thank you,' Alice heard Mrs Silbermann's relieved voice.

Alice too felt relieved. Soon they would be under the shower – clean at last, free to drink. The world turned black before her eyes and she felt her knees give way.

25

•••

When she came to she was immediately struck by the long rows of clothes' hooks. Then she became aware of the numbers beside the hooks. Each hook had a large, clear number.

'There,' said Ruth, patting her cheeks gently, 'there you are again. You got a bit too heavy for me, my dear, from out there to in here. If Rebekka and Aaron had not helped me . . .'

'No wonder she collapsed,' said the singer, stroking Alice's hair. Then she hung her coat up on a hook. There were Rebekka, David and Ruben too, beside Ruth, and Aaron behind Ruben. They were all smiling at her.

'Your colour will soon come back,' said the red-cheeked woman, who had also hung up her coat.

'Undress, undress,' came a voice. 'There's a lot more to go through today!'

Alice understood. So this was a cloakroom, and probably the shower-room was next door.

'*If* I hurry,' said the singer, 'it's only for the sake of the hot coffee.'

'Coffee?' said the red-cheeked woman. 'Are you sure?'

'Get undressed, children,' said Ruth, pulling her blouse over her head.

'In front of the children?' said the singer, giving Aaron an angry look.

'Let's look forward to the water,' said Ruth calmly. 'We all need it. It's only a shame that we can't wash our clothes at the same time. Once we're clean we shall have to get back into this filthy stuff again.'

The singer rolled down her stockings, the red-cheeked woman stepped out of her dress, and somewhere in the next row Alice heard the Silbermann girls whispering and giggling. A baby was crying. 'Come here, Benni!' came the blonde woman's voice.

Alice was still dazed. Slowly she pulled off her shoes, still crusted with muck. How they stank! She hung up her coat on one of the hooks that was still free. One hundred and seventy-three. One, seven, three. It would be too silly if afterwards she had to wander about naked among all these naked people, looking for her clothes

'Tie your shoes together,' said Ruth, pointing to the wall, where the instruction was written up in large letters. It also said that the clothes were to be arranged tidily – and it actually said so in several languages!

'They have thought of everything,' Alice heard Mrs Silbermann say.

Ruth was already naked, and now Alice also dared to pull off her dress. She would not be the first naked person in the room. How difficult it was, in front of so many people . . . Never, not since she could remember, had she been naked in front of anyone but her parents and grandparents.

She glanced sideways at Rebekka, who was also naked and had arranged her clothes tidily. Now Rebekka was undoing her plaits. That was a good idea: their hair was in great need of a wash. Alice pulled the ends of wool out of her plaits and put them in her shoes. Her plaits were springing loose on their own, but she helped them along with nervous fingers.

The singer beside her was also completely undressed. How creased her legs were, and how slack her breasts. Alice scarcely dared to look, but now she had to, for out of her bag the singer took a tiny bottle, opened it and dabbed herself behind both ears and between her breasts.

'Why don't you put it off until afterwards?' asked a strange woman. 'The water will wash it all away.'

'You feel less naked with it on,' said the singer. She handed Alice the bottle and said, 'Here, you cover yourself in lilac too.'

Alice dabbed, and a wonderful scent of lilac floated round them. Suddenly it no longer seemed so very bad having to undress in front of other people. Zip-zip, everything off, folded up – done. Now only the locket was left. The singer was also wearing a locket round her neck.

'They evidently don't think we need a mirror,' she said, opening her handbag, which was hanging on the hook. She took out a hand-mirror and looked at herself. 'Unrecognizable,' she sighed. 'After the shower I shall need a long time for my toilette.' She tugged at her chain and her golden earrings.

'Hurry up, Ruben,' said Ruth, helping David to take off his shoes. He had knotted his shoelaces and Alice could see that Ruth's fingers were trembling.

The room was beginning to empty. One woman after another, many with children, some without, disappeared into the shower-room through a big door in the background.

Alice suddenly remembered the jewel case. She tugged it out of her coat pocket, opened it hastily and looked inside. Yes, there they were, the beautiful chains and collars, the bracelets and earrings which had trickled through her fingers so many times – and which she had so often put on and admired in the basement bathroom mirror.

'*Oh, là là*!' said the singer, her voice hushed. 'Have you any idea what you've got there, child? They belonged to your mother, didn't they?'

Alice nodded.

The singer looked anxiously round. 'I would not leave those here while we're in the shower,' she whispered. 'You never know if the supervisors can be trusted.' Her gold tooth flashed.

'But what shall I do with them?' asked Alice.

'Put them all on,' whispered the singer. 'If you're wearing them, they can't get lost.'

She was already putting one necklace after another round Alice's neck, holding out the open bracelets to her, closing the fastenings and slipping on the rings. They were too big, so she pushed them on to Alice's thumb.

'Some people do have problems.' said Ruth indignantly.

One necklace of shining green beads reached almost to Alice's knees, dangling uncomfortably against her thighs, so the singer arranged the necklace in a fourfold crown and pressed it down on her hair.

'Look' she said, handing her the glass.

Alice saw a bright, smiling face, a good face. And the green necklace shimmering on her forehead looked beautiful.

'Leave all that frippery,' urged Ruth. 'We are almost the last.'

There was no time left for the earrings. Alice dropped them back in the jewel case and put it in her coat pocket.

26

•••

In the shower-room the naked bodies of the women and children were already crowded together. Alice could see them through the open door. Even before she was inside the room herself, she realized that there would be very little room for showering. How pale their bodies were – and in high summer!

'Will those few nozzles be enough for all of us?' she heard Ruth wondering. Then she was pushed forward by the people coming in behind her.

Alice glanced up at the ceiling. There really were not many nozzles – not nearly enough for so many people. But perhaps they squirted in all directions and sprayed over a wide area?

'I'm so thirsty,' grumbled David.

'Open your mouth while you shower,' said Ruben. He waved across at Walter Maibaum and his brothers.

Suddenly Alice felt something wet running down the inside of her thigh. She bent forward and turned her leg outward. It was blood.

Ruth put her arm round Alice and Alice saw that her eyes

had filled with tears. With trembling fingers, Alice opened her locket and pressed her lips to the pictures of her parents.

Then another door creaked open on the far side of the room, and in swarmed a crowd of naked men. They were followed by two or three men in striped clothes and a man in uniform, who stood by the door. The women shrank back, shocked, and the room grew even more cramped.

'Perhaps my father and brothers are there,' cried Aaron, pushing his way towards the men.

'Don't forget your number,' Ruben shouted after him.

'Incredible,' Alice heard the singer gasp. 'They treat us like animals!'

Alice was quite calm now. After the shower she would drink coffee with the grown-ups . . .

She looked around for Aaron. Up to now, she had seen naked men only in Grandfather's art books. Aaron was beautiful – Paul would certainly have been even more beautiful.

Aaron was pushing his way back, looking dejected. He had obviously not found his father and brother. Alice waved to him. She saw the uniformed man and the men in stripes leaving the room. The heavy iron door slammed shut.

Alice tipped back her head. Soon, soon, water would pour down over her from the nozzle up there. The water of life. It would wash her clean of the dirt and horror of the journey, would make her as clean as she had been before. She raised her arms and opened out her hands.

Afterword

•••

The Nazi regime led by Adolf Hitler came to power in Germany in the 1930s. The regime dealt brutally with all forms of opposition.

In 1938 Hitler declared that 'one of these days the Jews will disappear from Europe' and in Germany and occupied Europe his regime began systematically to round up Jewish people and transport them to concentration camps. Auschwitz in Eastern Europe was one of the camps. In the camps, special equipment for mass murder had been set up, including gas chambers disguised as showers.

On arrival at the camps the prisoners underwent a 'selection' process. Those fit enough to work became slave labourers and worked in terrible conditions until they died. The rest – the young, the old, women with small children, people with disabilities and the sick – were selected for immediate extermination in the gas chambers. Six million Jews died in what has become known as the Holocaust, along with thousands of gypsies, homosexuals, people with disabilities and dissidents of all kinds.